Hannah & Harley

AKA H & H Investigations

CHRISTY WILBURN NOBELLA WEBB

STRATTON
—PRESS—
Publishing Life

Hannah & Harley AKA H & H Investigations
Copyright © 2020 **Christy Wilburn Nobella Webb**

All rights reserved. No part of this book may be used or reproduced by any means, graphic, electronic, or mechanical, including photocopying, recording, taping or by information storage and retrieval system without the written permission of the author except in the case of brief quotations embodied in critical articles and reviews.

Stratton Press Publishing
831 N Tatnall Street Suite M #188,
Wilmington, DE 19801
www.stratton-press.com
1-888-323-7009

Because of the dynamic nature of the Internet, any web addresses or links contained in this book may have changed since publication and may no longer be valid. The views expressed in the work are solely those of the author and do not necessarily reflect the views of the publisher, and the publisher hereby disclaims any responsibility for them.

ISBN (Paperback): 978-1-64895-130-5
ISBN (Ebook): 978-1-64895-131-2

Printed in the United States of America

Dedicated to my beloved cat, Harley, who was my constant companion for sixteen years and who inspired me to write this series. I miss you, dear kitty!
To Rocky, my brave Saint Bernard and protector!

Chapter 1

1999, South Jordan, Utah

Hannah pushed the exit door open and hungrily breathed in the October air on her way out of the office building, hoping and praying she had just made a good impression at her job interview. She couldn't believe she had been out of work now for over two months, with no prospects on the horizon because she had too much work experience. Didn't these people know she was getting desperate? If she heard one more person tell her that they were sure she would find a job soon because of her qualifications and work experience, she would scream! Her nest egg of savings was almost gone, and if she didn't get hired soon, she was sure her home would be the next item on the chopping block.

She had relocated from California to Utah two years ago after the death of her husband when an opening for a manager in a retail store had been posted. Having grown up in Utah as a child, it seemed like the perfect time to return and start fresh with the hope of making new memories…and possibly finding love again. It came as quite a shock to her when the area manager announced that the company had decided to close its doors, not being able to compete with the larger chain stores that were moving into the area. To complicate matters further, she wasn't even given a severance package and was given a week's notice to close the store. She was in her fifties now; however, she was often told by her peers that she didn't look her age. She was beginning to have her doubts about that when she couldn't get anyone to hire her.

Climbing into her car, she took a long look in the vanity mirror, which was positioned in front of her, to check out her appearance. Her strawberry-blonde hair was shoulder length and was a little blonder now due to the gray hair that was competing to take over. Her eyes were large, with a deep sapphire tinge to them that tended to give away her every emotion. She sighed with disgust as she saw the sprinkling of freckles covering her face. Her mother had promised they would disappear by the time she was grown up. Smiling, she couldn't help thinking, *I must not be grown up yet!* She closed the mirror and started her car, wondering which was louder, the roar of her car engine or her stomach growling in protest from not enough food. Prior to losing her job, she had been wanting to lose a few extra pounds, but had never dreamed she would be forced to go on the diet she was currently on. The only way to describe it was to call it a survival diet in order to stretch her meager savings! It must be working because her friends at church and work had complimented her on her weight loss and wanted to know her secret. Wouldn't they be surprised if they really knew? She had cut back to eating one good meal a day and was snacking on little bites of fruit and nuts to keep her energy from running out the rest of the day. Even she had to admit it was working because she had had to dig around in the back of her closet to find a smaller size to wear to her interview. A year ago, she had debated about giving the smaller clothes to Goodwill, conceding she would never lose the weight. She was glad now that she hadn't done so.

Rolling down the window, she welcomed the autumn breeze while enjoying the gorgeous fall weather on her drive home. The leaves were dressed in their bright orange and red colors, with a variety of golden shades intermingled. It brought back vivid memories of walking home from school as a child, and she could even hear the distinct crunching of the leaves when her shoes made contact with them. A benefit of her limited budget was it enabled her to appreciate all the things that she normally took for granted. She was sure if she was still working, she would be too preoccupied to think about the leaves crunching beneath her feet or the finery of the fall leaves apparel.

After arriving home, she was met by her loyal cat, Harley. He was a large gray Maine coon, who was her constant companion and a gift from her deceased husband. He loved to eat and prided himself on being large yet very gentle and sociable. When children came to the door selling things, Harley always accompanied her. She couldn't help chuckling when the children would gawk in amazement at his size and cautiously ask if he was a dog, followed immediately by whether or not he would bite. Hannah enjoyed teasing them by stating, "He only eats children who are selling things and those that insult him by thinking he is a dog."

"Hello, Harley dog," Hannah greeted, thinking back on memories of her children and their friends calling him Harley dog due to his enormous size.

"Meow," he responded in a friendly tone while rubbing his large head against her leg.

"I just got back from my umpteenth interview. Boy, will I be glad when I get a job and don't have to go on any more of these interviews! Do you know what I mean?"

"Meow, meow," Harley responded.

"I knew you would. What have you been doing while I was gone? I hope you had a chance to vacuum and dust, and at least get some wash started."

Harley meowed, swishing his glorious tail back and forth against her legs.

"I'm guessing that means you were too busy taking a nap. In my next life, I'm definitely coming back as you, Harley. You've got it made!"

Bending down, Hannah lovingly scratched his ears and checked his food bowl to make sure he had plenty of food and water while she looked to see if the light on her answering machine was blinking, indicating any new messages. Trying not to get discouraged when she realized no one had called, she climbed the stairs to her bedroom to make her bed, which had been neglected in her hurry to be on time for her job interview.

While pulling the sheets and blankets into place, she thought about her interview. One of the challenges she was facing was the fact that she was trying to get out of the retail market and move into a field of work that was hopefully a little more stable. She wouldn't miss working weekends and holidays, which the retail world required, and hoped to find a job with business hours of eight to five. The working world had changed over the years, and she was quickly learning that it really wasn't what you knew anymore but who you knew that played a larger part in obtaining a job. She was fortunate to have a sister, Constance, who happened to hear about a job opening and talked to her friend, Lynn, who knew the manager. Lynn had pulled some strings, and that's how she was able to get the interview.

The new job was still related to the retail world; however, she had interviewed for the position of receptionist in the operations headquarters. If she got the job, she would be answering phones for the western division and felt sure she could impress them with her work ethics and hopefully after a suitable amount of time, transfer into another position where she could get an increase in pay. The salary she would start out with would barely cover the basics, including her mortgage, utilities, and a little food; however, she was determined to make it work. She just had to get a job before her money ran out.

Harley interrupted her thoughts with a mournful "meow," bringing Hannah out of her reverie.

"I'm sorry, Harley. You caught me worrying again, didn't you?"

"Meow."

"If I don't get this job, you're going to have to go on the same diet I'm on."

"Meow, meow!"

Hannah couldn't help laughing at his response. "I know what you mean—double meow!!" If she didn't know better, she was sure he could understand her every word. "Let me change my clothes and then we'll go downstairs and see what mischief we can get into."

Harley was very attentive and always tried to outguess her every move. When she started toward the stairs, he darted ahead, racing her to the bottom. "Hey you, slow down to fifty miles an hour. Are you trying to kill me?" She giggled. He always liked to have the last word, and she smiled when she heard his quick "meow" in response.

Opening the refrigerator, she reached into the crisper for a large red apple. When she sliced it, she heard its crunchy crispness as it fell open on the cutting board. While cutting away the core, her mouth began to water as she anticipated eating her first bite. One thing about this diet she was on, it helped her appreciate every morsel of food she was able to place in her mouth. Putting the rest of the pieces in a baggie, she headed to her sewing room to relax and work on a cross-stitch project. Since being alone, she had tried to keep several projects on hand that she enjoyed doing to help chase the blues away whenever they would suddenly try to make an appearance.

Checking the time, she realized it was time for *Judge JoJo*. She loved sewing while she watched the litigants plead their cases to the judge. "Too bad I didn't go to law school and become a judge, or even an attorney. I think I could have done well in that field," she mumbled during the commercials.

"Meow," Harley agreed.

"Why, thank you, Harley. I'm flattered that you think I would be good too."

"Meow…meow."

"Did you really mean what you just said, Harley? You would like me to start an investigation business, and you would be my partner?"

"Meow."

"I'll give it some thought, but it does take money, and right now we barely have enough to feed the two of us."

"Meow."

"You're right, I certainly won't give up on the idea. I'll just keep it on the backburner for now until I get a job and things are a little more stable around here…agreed?" Hannah smiled at Harley when she heard his steady purr but couldn't help thinking about his idea of starting an investigation company. If she did get the job she interviewed for today, she would have to get another part-time job in order to have any money for emergencies. It actually sounded like an intriguing idea, and Harley wasn't just any ordinary cat!

Chapter 2

A week had gone by, and Hannah still hadn't heard anything from Mr. Brown, the man she had interviewed with. She didn't want to annoy him; however, she needed to know how to move forward. Rehearsing several times what she would say to him, she dialed his number and breathed deeply while trying to stay calm.

"Hello, Mr. Brown. This is Hannah North. Thank you so much for taking my call. I wanted to follow up on my recent interview with your company to see if you've made a decision yet, or if you needed any further information from me."

"Hello, Hannah! It's good to hear from you. I apologize for not having had an opportunity to get back to you. We have selected you for the position, but before I can extend an offer, we are doing a background check on you due to the information you will have access to in your new position."

"Oh, that's great news, Mr. Brown. May I ask how long the background check will take?"

"We usually have them back by now, so after we hang up, I will give our HR Department a call to see where the holdup is. When I hear back from them, I will be able to extend an offer to you at that time."

"Thank you, Mr. Brown, for all you are doing. Today is Tuesday. If I don't hear back from you by Thursday, may I give you a call back Thursday afternoon for another update?"

"Yes, that will work, Hannah. Thank you for calling and following up. Goodbye for now."

Hannah's legs were trembling, and she decided she better sit down before she collapsed. Harley had been watching her very closely and couldn't help asking, "Meow?"

"It's good news, Harley, at least I think it is. They are waiting for a background check to come back on me, and once they have it, if all is in order, they will extend an offer…and I will finally have a job!"

"Meow, meow."

"You're right, Harley. Thank goodness for that."

"Meow."

"No, I haven't forgotten about your idea of an investigation company where you will help me solve cases and we can earn some extra money for emergencies. In fact, there was a flyer on the front porch for a neighborhood watch meeting tonight where they plan to discuss the vandalism of our neighbor's mailboxes. I was thinking this might be a case for H & H Investigations."

"Meow?"

"Oh, didn't I tell you? 'H & H Investigations' stands for 'Hannah & Harley Investigations.' What do you think?"

"Meow, meow."

"I thought you would like it. Now if we're really going to do this, you're going to have to start taking your naps with one eye open so you can start watching what's going on in the neighborhood while I'm working and especially keep an eye on what's going on after dark. You know what I mean?"

"Meow!"

"Good! I love your enthusiasm, Harley! I can tell already, we're going to make a great team!"

"Meow!"

The neighborhood watch meeting was being held at the Balls' home, who lived at the end of Hannah's street. She arrived five minutes early hoping to get in on any conversations regarding the damaged mailboxes before the meeting started.

"Hello, Hannah. It's nice that you could join us. You're not usually able to come to these meetings, so it's great to have you here," Emily Ball greeted her when she saw Hannah step inside.

"Thank you, Emily." Hannah would have normally sat by herself, but if she was serious about starting an investigation company, she needed to be assertive and decided she better sit where she could get a scoop on what was happening. "Do you mind if I join you two?" Hannah asked two of her neighbors who were in deep conversation.

"No, have a seat." Sally smiled and patted the chair next to hers.

"Have your mailboxes been damaged?" Hannah asked with concern.

"Yes," they both replied in unison.

"Has yours been hit yet, Hannah?" Martha asked.

"No, not yet."

"Well, how did you get so lucky?" Sally asked. "You may be the only one on our streets who hasn't been hit yet."

"Would you mind telling me what happened to each of you?" Hannah inquired.

"Well, I'm sure someone swung a baseball bat at mine because the box was knocked off of its pole and was halfway down the next block by the time we finally found it," Martha informed her disgustedly.

"Mine was most likely hit with a baseball bat too, but fortunately the box was just a few houses down when we found it," Sally advised.

"What time of day do you think it happened?" Hannah asked curiously.

"It must be happening sometime between midnight and five in the morning," Sally replied. "I have a couple of daughters who arrived home from dates around midnight and reported that our mailbox was fine when they got home."

"Welcome to our homeowners' meeting tonight," Emily Ball greeted, interrupting the conversations around the room. "It's a shame we have to meet under these circumstances, but it's always a good time to get to know each other a little better. As you are all aware, we have been experiencing vandalism in our neighborhood, and we are anxious to get it stopped before it gets out of hand. I'd like to open this meeting up to anyone who would like to share what's happened at their home, and any suggestions on what we can do about this situation are welcome."

The next half hour was filled with frustrated comments on what had happened to the individual homeowners; however, no one had any solutions on how to get the situation under control. Finally Art, who lived a few doors down from Hannah, suggested, "I think we should hire someone to patrol the area."

"How do we know they would be trustworthy, and it could get very expensive?" several homeowners asked. After listening to several discussions, Hannah raised her hand.

"I would like to offer a suggestion. I have started a small investigation company and would be willing to look into this situation without being paid until I have either solved the case or provided some concrete answers on who is doing this damage to our homes."

The room was silent for a few moments until a curious neighbor asked, "Just how would you go about it? Do you work alone or what?"

"That is a very good question, sir. However, I am not able to disclose what I do or who I work with. The less you know, the better it is for the success of my investigation. I can tell you that I have a very reliable partner who can get information in a very uncanny"—*or should I say uncatty,* she thought to herself—"way without our culprits ever suspecting."

Hannah looked around the room and noticed the stares from her neighbors. Up to this moment in time, she had always been a quiet neighbor who went about her business in a very private way, making it a point to never draw attention to herself.

"I suggest that we take a vote unless someone else has another suggestion," Emily stated.

The room remained silent, so Emily asked, "All in favor of Hannah's suggestion, raise your hand. Any opposed? Well, Hannah, it looks like the room is willing to give you a chance. I would also like to ask that everyone, if possible, make a donation to the jar I will leave on the table, and the money collected will be used to pay Hannah if she turns up anything. Why don't we meet back here in a month or sooner, depending on what you are able to come up with?"

"Thank you, Emily. I look forward to giving you some answers and returning our neighborhood back to its pristine state," Hannah answered with confidence.

* * * * *

"Harley, it's official! We have our first case," Hannah announced when she walked into the house after returning from the homeowners' meeting.

"Meow?"

"Well…it seems our first case involves mailboxes. Every mailbox on our street except ours has been damaged. The neighbors believe someone has been hitting them with a baseball bat, and they're doing it between midnight and five in the morning."

"Meow, meow."

"I agree with you, Harley. It does sound like it's probably teenagers. Here's what I think we need to do."

After reviewing several options together, Hannah was in awe of Harley's ingenious ideas and the resources he was already putting together. "Well, I think we're as ready as we're going to be. When are you going to talk to the horses across the street and the other cats that roam the neighborhood?"

"Meow."

"Okay, Harley, just be careful when you cross the street. I couldn't bear it if anything bad happened to you."

"Meow, meow."

"Now that we have everything settled, I guess we just watch and wait. I have to admit, I'm a little giddy and nervous."

"Meow."

"I'm glad you're not, Harley. One of us has to be cool, calm, and collected. I think I'll get ready for bed. All this detective stuff has made my head hurt, and I'm pretty tired."

"Meow."

"Okay, you take the first watch…and I'll leave the living room blinds slightly open for you. Wake me up if anything happens that I need to know about."

"Meow."

Chapter 3

Hannah woke up earlier than normal the following morning and hurried downstairs to see how Harley was faring. When she spotted him, she observed that he was sitting on top of the couch in a perched position, while staring out the window watching for anything that looked unusual or strange. Surprisingly, he still appeared very alert, and she cautiously asked, "How did your first night on duty go, Harley?"

"Meow, meow."

"Sounds like you had a pretty boring night, which is good and bad."

"Meow."

"I guess these things take time, not like the detective shows we watch on TV where they're solved in an hour. It's also a weeknight, and I bet a lot of the vandalism occurs on the weekends."

Harley followed her into the kitchen and watched her open a can of mixed nuts. While deep in thought and munching on a handful of nuts, she jumped when the telephone interrupted her thoughts. Hurrying to check the caller ID, she saw that the call was coming from Mr. Brown at Security Systems Inc. "Hello, this is Hannah speaking."

"Good morning, Hannah. This is Mr. Brown giving you a call back. Is this a good time to talk?"

"Yes, it is," Hannah answered hopefully.

"HR got your background check back and everything is in order, so I'm prepared now to make you an offer. Are you still interested in coming to work?"

"Yes, Mr. Brown, I would love to come to work for Security Systems Inc."

"We will start you at the salary we discussed at your interview, and we're hoping you can begin working on Monday morning at eight."

"That sounds great, Mr. Brown. I look forward to seeing you on Monday."

Hannah placed the phone back into its cradle and then did a happy dance while Harley watched with interest. "I got the job, Harley! We will have a steady income now, but we still need our investigation company to help supplement our income, okay?"

"Meow, meow."

"I was thinking over the next few days before I go back to work, we should come up with some signals in case we get into a jam and we can't talk to each other. Do you know what I mean, Harley?"

"Meow."

"I'm also going to climb up into the attic and find my dad's binoculars in case we get into a situation where I might need them to watch you. Before I do that, I'm going to go and take my shower and get dressed. You should take a nap, Harley. I can see that you're having a difficult time keeping your eyes open."

"Meow."

* * * * *

Hannah was putting the ladder back in the garage when she told Harley it was time to meet for a few minutes. "Look what I found, Harley, my dad's binoculars!"

Harley looked very impressed and rewarded her with a "meow."

"I'm hoping you had a chance to think of some signals we can use to help each other while we're working as detectives in case we get into a situation where we can't talk out loud to each other."

"Meow, meow."

Hannah listened and studied Harley closely while he showed her what he had come up with. "I am so impressed with you, Harley! You think of everything. I'm going to grab my notebook and write them down so I don't forget what you've told me."

After she returned to the room, she began writing down the signals as Harley once again demonstrated them. "Okay, so when you whip your tail back and forth, that means you are on to something and don't disturb you, you've got it handled. When you pull both ears back, you are in trouble and need my help ASAP. When you 'meow' three times, you are telling me who did the crime and I should call the police. Finally, you may use your paw to point anything out that is important or needs my attention. Harley, you are the most extraordinary cat I know!"

"Meow."

The doorbell rang, interrupting their conversation, and Hannah wondered out loud, "I wonder who that could be?" Hurrying to the door, she opened it to see a teenage boy holding an empty water cooler bottle that was filled with a couple of dollars and some change.

"Hello, ma'am. I am collecting whatever change you can spare for my high school to help feed the hungry in our area and was hoping you would be able to help out with a donation."

Before she could answer, Harley let out a warning growl, which he only did on occasions when he felt extremely threatened or vulnerable.

"W-wow…I've never seen or heard a cat do that," the teenager stammered while slowly backing away. "Is he going to attack me or what?"

Looking down at Harley, she noticed that he was whipping his tail back and forth, and she remembered it to be his signal letting her know he was on to something. She wondered if the teenager was the one vandalizing the mailboxes, or maybe he was a decoy while his friends were casing potential homes to target next. Just then the telephone rang, and Harley let out another warning growl, acting even more agitated while continuing to whip his tail back and forth. When Harley began advancing toward the front door, that was enough to scare the teenager off, and he turned to run in the opposite direction.

"Don't worry about a donation," he called over his shoulder. "I'll come back later if we need it!"

"Wow, that was bizarre!" Hannah stated as she moved to go and answer the phone. Halfway there, it stopped ringing. "Now who do you suppose that was? If I didn't know better, I would say our house was next on the target list. What do you think, Harley?"

"Meow…meow!"

"So you came to the same conclusion? I haven't heard you growl like that since we first moved here and you looked out the window and saw horses for the first time! You even scared me when you growled! What made you growl like that today, Harley?"

"Meow…meow."

"Wow, I'm so glad you had a talk with the horses across the street and they told you to watch for a guy with a big plastic bottle. It's nice to have more than one set of eyes helping us! That smarty-pants teenager thinks he's so cool, and he doesn't even have a clue who's on to him! That was a good idea to growl. It definitely let him know he's not just dealing with any ordinary cat!"

"Meow."

"For sure we better keep our eyes and ears open on him and his possible gang of friends—if he has one, right?"

"Meow."

* * * * *

"You guys would not believe what just happened to me," Pete said while trying to catch his breath. "I went to the house on the corner, and the biggest cat I've ever seen started growling at me. He looked like he was going to rip me up one side and down the other! I didn't wait around for a donation, I just got out of there! I'm not kidding! There's something creepy about that cat!"

"Ohhh…is poor little Petey scared of a kitten?"

"You watch what you're saying, Dirk. I dare you to go over there!"

"Come on, you two...let's stay focused. Count your money. I want to see how much we were able to collect today," Bill ordered. The group of guys had gathered around a table at a nearby park, and he watched as they dumped the money from their plastic bottles and began counting.

"So it looks like we were able to collect just a little over fifty dollars. Not bad...but not good enough. If we're going to have enough money to split between us so we don't have to worry about working, we've got to do a heck of a lot better than that. We're going to have to take out a few more mailboxes and then leave notes on people's doors advising them if they want the damage to stop, they're going to have to pay by leaving money in an envelope at a specified drop-off point."

Pete checked his watch and looked at Bill. "I've got to get going so I don't arouse suspicion coming home late."

"Yeah...we wouldn't want your mommy to put you in time-out!" Dirk said while trying to control his laughter.

"Dirk, I said that was enough. We all need to stay focused if we're going to pull this thing off."

"Are we going to hit more mailboxes this weekend?" Craig asked.

"No, I think we need to back off for a few weeks so the neighbors begin to relax and then we'll hit it hard again...and they'll be more likely to cooperate when we request money to get us to stop," Bill advised.

Chapter 4

The weekend passed by quietly; however, Harley and Hannah kept a steady vigil for any untoward activities. Hannah hadn't slept very well Sunday night, trying to be alert for any vandalism that might occur, and of course, the anticipation of starting her new job had kept her adrenaline pumping.

"I'm ready to go to work now, Harley. I'm counting on you to keep an eye on things, and I've left your kitty door unlocked if you need to go outside to check on anything. I'll try to come home for lunch, but I can't guarantee it. With this being my first day on the job, I'm not sure what to expect."

"Meow."

"Thanks for understanding. I'll fill you in on all the details when I get home. You be careful. Love you!"

"Meow."

While driving through the neighborhood on her way to work, she checked her neighbor's yards for anything that looked amiss. So far, so good. She couldn't help thinking about the teenager who had stopped by to get a donation. Maybe he was legit…who knew? She also wondered where he lived. Did he live in her neighborhood? She made a mental note to check on him later. Maybe Harley could check with the animals in the neighborhood to find out if he was a local kid or from another area.

It didn't take long to get to work, a quick ten minutes using side streets. The gas she would save on commuting to work would definitely be a plus. She grabbed her belongings and rushed inside, breathing deeply to help compose her nerves. She felt like crossing her fingers for good luck while inwardly praying this new job would be one she'd enjoy.

Now that she was an employee of Security Systems, she took a closer look at the office she would be spending a good deal of time in. The walls were painted in a light gray color, and the pictures hanging on them were scenes of Utah's gorgeous mountains. The reception area was small but accommodating, with several chairs and a couch gathered around a coffee table with magazines to keep potential clients occupied while they waited for their appointments. The desk that she would be working at was placed strategically in the room for easy access in directing clients in and out of the office.

Rachel, the receptionist she would be replacing, guided her around to the four offices down the hallway and introduced her to the employees she would be working with. Everyone was welcoming, and she was beginning to slowly relax while feeling relief at finally having obtained a job.

* * * * *

The morning flew by, and Hannah couldn't believe it was lunchtime when she walked outside to get into her car. She had spent the majority of her morning filling out the new-hire paperwork, as well as getting acquainted with several of the employees she would be working with. Those she had talked to treated her kindly, and she felt that she would fit in well. Of course, once she got all the names and job titles committed to memory, answering the phone would be a breeze.

She thought about the coincidence of starting her own detective business while simultaneously beginning a new job at a security systems company that could potentially work hand in hand with her future cases and couldn't help smiling. Pulling into her garage, she wondered how Harley's day had gone.

Harley waited patiently at the door to greet Hannah. "How's my Harley dog?" Hannah asked.

"Meow...meow?"

"My morning went good, and so far, I like my job. Thanks for asking, Harley. How was your morning?"

"Meow."

"I'm glad it was a slow morning for you, Harley, because I need you to talk to some of the animals in the neighborhood to see if they know where that teenager lives. Also, would you mind asking them if they've seen any other kids with plastic bottles that might be part of his gang?"

"Meow."

"You're the best, Harley! I love your positive attitude." Hannah hurried over to a cupboard to reward Harley with some of his favorite cat treats.

"I think I'll have my main meal after work. I'm not that hungry right now. I'll cut up an apple to take back with me just in case I get hungry. If I hurry, I can catch half of *Judge JoJo*. Do you want to join me, Harley?"

"Meow!"

* * * * *

The afternoon passed by as quickly as the morning had, and Hannah was feeling happy with her new job. She was getting more efficient at transferring the phone calls when they came in, and Mr. Brown had brought over some literature for her to study between phone calls to help educate her on their security systems. She had had a nice conversation with one of the top salesmen for the company and had asked him if he had any advice for her if she decided to join the sales department. He had said one thing that had stood out in her mind, "Knowledge equals money. The more you know, the better you can sell the product."

She thought his answer definitely had merit and brought some of the product brochures home to study. When she turned into her driveway, she was happy once again that her drive back home didn't take long and couldn't wait to see if Harley had any more information on the teenagers.

"Hello, Harley! I'm anxious to hear how your afternoon went and if you were able to find out any more about that teenager."

"Meow...meow...meow!"

"Excellent, Harley! So, the horses and the two cats down the street have seen at least three to four boys going through the neighborhood with large plastic bottles. Did they recognize any of them and know if they live in our area?"

"Meow."

"It figures that they all look like strangers. No one usually targets their own neighborhood in order to stay incognito." Hannah hurried upstairs to change her clothes, hoping it would be a quiet evening so she could get to bed early and catch up on the sleep she had missed the night before.

* * * * *

The work week flew by, and things stayed quiet on the home front. Hannah was grateful to have Harley for a partner because he didn't mind keeping watch over things at night.

Mr. Brown complimented her on a job well done as she was leaving for the weekend. She was relieved that she seemed to fit in well with the other employees, and each day the job of answering the phone was becoming easier.

Now if she and Harley could just figure out who was doing the damage to the mailboxes and earn a little extra money, that would be perfect! While sitting at a traffic light, she saw two boys entering the crosswalk. They were both carrying large plastic water bottles. They were deep into conversation, and she doubted that they had even noticed her. Keeping her eye on which direction they were going, she decided to follow them and hopefully discover where they lived or what neighborhood they were going to.

After driving through the intersection, she quickly changed lanes and made a U-turn so she could follow the boys. To avoid alerting them to her actions, she pulled over to the side of the road to give them time to stay ahead of her, not wanting to draw any attention. The boys were still in deep conversation and seemed totally unaware that she was following them. They turned onto a side street that lead to a park she didn't know existed in the area before today. Once again she pulled over to the side of the road, wishing she had brought her binoculars so she could watch them from a distance in order to try to figure out what they were up to. While waiting for them to move ahead, she made a mental note to keep her binoculars in the car from now on.

Just before the boys disappeared from her sight, she pulled away from the curb where she was parked and began slowly following them to discover where they were going. After a few seconds, she could see that they had joined two other boys at a park table and bench, and it looked like they were having some kind of a meeting. She wished she could hear what they were saying, but didn't dare move any closer, worried she would give herself away. After several more minutes had passed, she decided to rush home and grab Harley so he could get close enough to hear what they were talking about.

When Hannah came rushing into the house, it startled Harley, who was just waking up from a nap. He recovered quickly when she explained about the boys being up to something, and he hurried to follow her out the door, jumping quickly into the front seat. It didn't take long for them to return to the park, and with luck on their side, they found the boys still deep in conversation.

"You be careful, Harley. I'll be watching from the car through these binoculars so I can see whatever's going on."

"Meow."

Hannah's hands were shaking when she picked up the binoculars, and she held her breath as she observed Harley's approach toward the boys. He truly was a hunter, slithering forward while the boys were oblivious to his movements. She hadn't noticed the large tree before, with its enormous branches that reached high above the table where the boys were sitting. She watched in amazement as Harley scaled its height and climbed out onto a branch where he had a perfect view of the boys and was in a good position to hear whatever plans they were making. When the boys stood to leave, Hannah checked her watch and saw that they had been talking for at least a half hour when Harley had climbed the tree. The boys were now pairing up and began leaving, each duo in a different direction. When she saw two boys approaching her parked car, she pretended to be taking a nap as they strode by. Once they had walked a reasonable distance to not draw any attention to herself, Hannah opened the car door and raced to where Harley was climbing down from the tree.

"How did everything go, Harley? You sure looked amazing scrambling up that tree!"

"Meow…meow…meow."

Harley seemed to go on forever relaying the bits and pieces of the conversation he had just eavesdropped on. "Oh my goodness, Harley, I think we are on the right trail of the guys who have been vandalizing our neighborhood!"

"Meow!"

"It sounds like they have decided to lay low for a few weeks and then start up again catching everybody off guard. Can you believe their audacity to leave notes requesting money to pay them to stop destroying property?"

"Meow…meow!"

"I agree! They have a lot of nerve! Well, hopefully they have met their match and we can catch them in the act and stop their vandalism."

"Meow."

"That's another good point, Harley. Who would have thought that while they are collecting money to help the hungry, they are really casing our neighbor's homes to see what they can steal? We have really got our work cut out for us!"

"Meow."

"The question now is, where and how do we proceed from here? Do you have any suggestions, Harley?"

"Meow…meow."

"I'm not sure either. Our biggest challenge is finding out when they are going to make their next move." As Hannah drove home, she was in deep thought when Harley interrupted her thoughts with a "meow."

"I'm sorry, Harley. Would you mind saying that again?"

"Meow…meow."

"I think you're right. For now, we need the horses, the two cats down the street, and what do you think about involving the Saint Bernard, Rocky, who lives a few doors down from us?"

"Meow."

"I know you don't like Rocky slobbering on everything, but it could come in handy if he were to slime some of the bad guys if we got in a real jam while trying to catch these guys."

"Meow…meow."

"I thought you would see it that way." Hannah laughed. "It doesn't hurt that he's very big and powerful! I wouldn't want to be tackled by a Saint Bernard and then slimed on top of that!"

"Meow."

"I know it's disgusting, Harley, but if it helps us, we need to consider all of our options."

"Meow."

"Okay, I'm glad you're in agreement. I need you to talk to your friends and get them watching and listening so we can figure out when these juveniles are going to make their next move. Once we have an idea, we can make our plans, catch them, and collect a paycheck from our neighborhood watch group."

"Meow."

"You're right, that definitely means more cat treats!"

Chapter 5

Hannah stood and stretched, happy to have finished reading the last product brochure she had brought home for the weekend, and stacked it neatly on top of the other brochures she had studied. She was definitely getting an education on the security systems her company offered and knew she could be a lot more effective at answering all the questions that would come her way when answering the phones. She hoped it would make a good impression on Mr. Brown too, and he would want to transfer her to a sales position where she could make more money.

Her stomach growled, reminding her that it was time for her meal of the day, and she licked her lips in anticipation when she thought about the pork chops she had purchased the previous day at the grocery store. As she prepared the pork chops, she fondly remembered her husband's excitement over grinding up a bag of garlic-and-butter-flavored croutons and smiled when she thought about him rolling the pork chops in the freshly ground crumbs while whistling a favorite tune. Oh, how she missed him and loved the memories that would always have a cherished place in her heart.

She placed the two pork chops that were now rolled into the crumb mixture carefully into a greased cooking dish just as the oven began beeping, letting her know it had reached the baking temperature. While the pork chops baked, she made a tossed salad with lettuce and her favorite bits of chopped cabbage, cucumbers, shredded carrots, tomatoes, and celery, with a sprinkling of sharp cheese on top. She quickly set the table and pulled the new light Thousand Island dressing she had purchased out of the refrigerator. With only a few minutes left to go on the pork chops, she decided to dig into her tossed salad. The flavors melted in her mouth, and if she didn't know better, she would have believed she was in one of Utah's finest restaurants.

As she ate her dinner, she was grateful to be working again and was happy to have a relaxing weekend without the worry of trying to hunt down a job. She was a little surprised that she and Harley hadn't seen the boys with their plastic bottles lately, and she'd even taken a walk around the block earlier in the day to see if all the neighborhood mailboxes were intact. Fortunately, everything seemed in order, and no one would have ever guessed they were having any problems with vandalism.

Emily Ball was in her front yard when Hannah had walked by, so she stopped to give her a brief update on her investigation. Emily was naturally curious on any information that Hannah could provide; however, she had to remind Emily it was still a little premature for her to share anything pertinent. Her thoughts were interrupted when she heard Harley enter the kitchen through his kitty door. "Hello, Harley dog! Any new developments on our case?"

"Meow…meow."

"Really? That would be an interesting twist, wouldn't it? Tell me more."

"Meow…meow…meow."

"So, if I heard you correctly, Fluffy overheard a couple of the bullies giving one of the boys named Pete a bad time?"

"Meow."

"I wonder which boy is Pete. Can you find out from Fluffy which boy is Pete?"

"Meow."

"If that's true, maybe we can get Pete on our side, and he could be an inside spy or ally for us. This is great news, Harley. I need you to find out by tomorrow which boy is Pete so we can make some plans."

"Meow…meow."

"Perfect, Harley. I think you deserve a treat, as well as, your dinner. Wouldn't you agree?"

"Meow!"

* * * * *

Hannah was rushing to get ready for work the following morning and for a brief moment, missed the days when she was unemployed and could just relax and take her time getting dressed. However, it only took a minute to remember the stress of those days wondering where her next house payment was going to come from to get her moving and grateful to have a job.

Before leaving for work, she called out to Harley, "Don't forget to check with Fluffy to see if you can find out which boy is Pete. I think it will really help our investigation if we could get him on our side. I will see you later, Harley."

As she backed her car out of the garage, she was glad she had put the brochures she had borrowed in the car the night before. It always amazed her how crazy things could get in the morning, and it was one less thing she had to worry about.

When Hannah pulled into the parking lot at work, she checked the clock on her dashboard and was relieved to see that she was eight minutes ahead of schedule. She quickly gathered the brochures and her purse and entered the building. It was nice to arrive ahead of the sales department because it gave her time to get the office lights turned on, the copy machines turned on and stocked with paper, and of course, a fresh pot of coffee brewing for the employees and any visitors that might like a cup.

Hannah heard the front door open and looked up to see Kyle walking in. "Good morning, Kyle. I wanted to let you know I had a chance to study the brochures you suggested over the weekend, and I think it's going to really help me when I try to answer our customer's questions. Thank you for suggesting them."

"No problem, Hannah. I'm glad I could be of help," Kyle replied while heading to his office.

Hannah greeted Mr. Brown when he walked into the office and wanted to tell him about studying the brochures; however, the day had started and things were already getting hectic, making it impossible to have that conversation. Hopefully, the customers would just let him know how helpful and knowledgeable their new receptionist was, and she wouldn't even have to toot her own horn.

It was a gorgeous fall day with temperatures in the sixties when Hannah left the office to take her lunch hour. She couldn't wait to get home to talk to Harley to see if he had found out which boy was Pete.

"Hello, Harley! How was your morning?"

"Meow…meow!"

"Wow! Fantastic! So the boy that came to our house was Pete?"

"Meow."

"I'm not sure if I would recognize him again. Would you, Harley?"

"Meow!"

"Thank goodness! I sure am glad you're on my team. Can you give me a description of him?"

"Meow…meow."

"Okay…he has brown hair, blue eyes, a nice smile and a dimple in his chin?"

"Meow…meow."

"He's also about six feet tall with a slim build. I'm very proud of you that you were able to get all this information, Harley. Now we just have to keep our eyes open and be on the lookout so we can spot him. Let's go get you a treat, and I need to get me some nuts and an apple for lunch."

While Harley munched his treats, Hannah ate half of her apple slices along with a portion of her nuts. "Well, Harley, I only had time to watch half of *Judge JoJo*, and now I need to get back to work. I hope you have a good afternoon, and let's both keep a lookout for Pete, okay?"

"Meow."

* * * * *

The phones were extra busy, and Hannah couldn't believe the afternoon had flown by so quickly when she glanced at the clock and saw it was time to begin her closing procedures. She had to admit she was a little disappointed that the day had been so busy that she didn't have an opportunity to tell Mr. Brown about being able to study the brochures over the weekend. The important thing was she had noticed a big difference in her ability to answer more customer questions because of the time she had taken to study. Before leaving the office, she grabbed a few more brochures to study and headed out the door to the parking lot.

When she turned into her neighborhood, she noticed several of her neighbors were gathered in small groups, and they didn't appear to be very happy, based on their body language. Hannah took a closer look and noticed as she drove by several garage doors that there were large blobs of paint that looked like they were either splattered or thrown at the doors. "Oh boy, looks like our vandals have been up to some new pranks," Hannah muttered.

After pulling into her driveway, she parked her car and hurried over to the nearest group of people. "Looks like our vandals have been up to mischief again," Hannah said.

"You can say that again," Mark, one of the neighbors, replied angrily.

"Once more, Hannah, it seems that your door is the only one that didn't get hit," Sally added suspiciously.

"Don't get me wrong," Hannah began to reply, "I'm not complaining, and I certainly don't have an answer on why my house is the only one that gets skipped. Do you think it's because my house is on the corner and it's more visible to someone who could call the police?"

"I suppose that's possible," Sally replied.

"I thought you was goin' to figure out who's doin' all this stuff? Isn't that what we're paying you for?" Art quickly interjected.

"If you remember from our meeting, I refused to take any money until I had an opportunity for my partner and I to do some investigating into this matter," Hannah answered.

"Well, what have you and your partner found out?" Art demanded.

"Unfortunately these things take time. We have narrowed a few things down and are in the process of devising a plan to catch the vandals as we speak," Hannah responded confidently.

Art rolled his eyes and muttered, "Apparently not fast enough."

Emily Ball walked up to the group in time to hear the last few comments. "I have full confidence in Hannah and her team, and after talking to her yesterday while she was walking around our neighborhood to check things out, she explained how she's working hard to get this situation resolved. We all promised to give her a chance, and I think we owe it to her to finish her investigation."

"Well, we can't wait forever and just sit back and let these hoodlums ruin our homes," Art sputtered.

Emily turned to Hannah and asked, "When do you think you'll have some answers and can meet to give us an update?"

Thinking quickly, Hannah said, "How about a week from this Wednesday? There have been some new developments that my team needs to follow up on, and we need the weekend to put our plan into action. I'm hoping by next Wednesday, we will have some culprits identified and a plan underway to catch them. Will that work for everyone?"

As Hannah studied the expressions on those that had gathered around, it seemed that the anger and frustration that was present earlier slowly began to dissipate. "The good thing about the paint they used on our garage doors is it's washable paint and fairly easy to remove with water from your hose, a rag, and a little elbow grease," Mark offered.

"That's one thing we can be thankful for," Emily said cheerfully.

The group continued to grumble and mumble, and Hannah decided it would be a good time to make her exit. "I'll catch all of you later," Hannah said, turning to walk home, hoping she would make it before things got heated again. All the way home, she hoped Harley hadn't slept through the latest fiasco and couldn't wait to talk to him to see what he knew.

Chapter 6

Harley was waiting anxiously for Hannah when she opened the kitchen door. "I'm glad you're here, Harley, and I'm really hoping you saw what went on around here today."

"Meow…meow…meow!"

"Whoa…slow down, Harley! You're talking, or should I say, meowing, too fast."

"Meow…meow."

"You're kidding me! Fluffy and Copper saw the boys who usually carry the plastic bottles, but this time they were carrying guns that shot paint?"

"MEOW…MEOW!"

"Oh no, Copper got his tail shot, and now half of his tail is yellow?"

"Meow!"

"I bet he's not happy about that."

"Meow…meow…meow!"

"Well, that's good news in a way, Harley. Because of what happened today, Copper is definitely ready to join our team and help us catch these bad boys. Now we just need to come up with a plan, and come up with it quick."

"Meow!"

"When I got home today, several of our neighbors were having a meeting, and Art is really mad and thinks we're not working fast enough."

"Growl….hiss…meow!"

"I know what you mean, Harley. He made me a little hot under the collar too! He's demanding that we have a meeting and give them some answers or they will probably want to hire someone else. Fortunately, Emily Ball stood up for us and is giving us until next Wednesday to have some concrete answers."

"Meow."

"By the way, did you think to ask Fluffy and Copper if Pete was with the group of boys today that were shooting paintballs?"

"Meow."

"It's okay, Harley. With all the excitement, that was probably the last thing on your mind. Would you go out right now and see if you can find out whether Pete was a part of that group?"

"Meow…meow."

"Thanks, Harley, and be careful."

"Meow."

Hannah watched Harley slip out the kitty door, run across the yard, and jump the vinyl fence in a single leap. While watching out the kitchen window, she was fascinated with his ability to maneuver whatever was in his pathway and reach his target without giving it a second thought. In her next life, she was definitely coming back as a cat. For now, she needed to come up with a plan of action that would stop these vandals in their tracks.

* * * * *

Several hours had gone by, and Harley still hadn't returned. Hannah was finishing her dinner dishes and was starting to worry about what could have happened to him. She made up her mind to give him about ten more minutes, and if he didn't come home, she was going to get in the car and start looking for him. Just when she thought she couldn't take it a minute longer, she heard him come through his kitty door.

"Oh, Harley, you had me worried sick! Are you all right? Where have you been?"

"Meow…meow."

"I'm sorry I can't help it. You know I can't bear to think of life without you!"

"Meow…meow."

"Okay, I'll relax. Tell me what you found out."

"Meow…meow…meow."

"Well, that makes sense. I'm sure Copper's mom was really upset to see his tail had been painted yellow, and she had to give him a bath before he could come outside. What did he have to say?"

"Meow…meow."

"Did you give Fluffy and Copper a description of Pete?"

"Meow."

"It sounds like he wasn't in the group that did the paintball shooting, which is good. The question now is, why wasn't he?"

"Meow."

"Somehow we have got to find him this week and talk to him to see if he really wants to stay involved with this gang of boys or if he is starting to have second thoughts."

"Meow…meow."

"I don't know about you, Harley, but all this detective stuff is making me tired. Let's get you some food, and of course a treat, and I'm going to go to bed early tonight."

"Meow."

"I really appreciate you taking over the night watch because I know I can't stay awake to do it. Good night, Harley, and thanks for all you do."

"Meow."

* * * * *

The workweek continued to fly by, and Hannah was getting concerned that she wasn't making any progress on her vandalism case. She had just gotten home from work, and while changing her clothes, an idea came to her that she felt impressed to check out.

"Harley, I'm going over to that park where we saw those boys having a meeting. For some reason, I have a feeling that Pete might be there, and I want to go and check it out."

"Meow…meow."

"I'll be careful, and if I'm not back by dark, you get Fluffy and Copper and come check on me, okay?"

"Meow."

Hannah gripped the steering wheel tightly as she drove cautiously over to the secluded park. *Please be there, Pete, and please be alone.* From a distance, she thought she could see someone sitting alone at the table when she parked her car. As she approached the table, the individual appeared to be leaning over while studying something or possibly even sleeping. She cleared her voice, hoping to get the attention of whomever was at the table.

"Hello there," Hannah called with a noticeable quiver in her voice.

Suddenly, the person sat up, and she could tell immediately it was a boy. His body language sent an immediate message that he didn't want to be bothered, and he scowled at her as she approached him cautiously.

"Are you Pete?" Hannah asked warily.

"Who wants to know?" Pete growled back.

"A friend," Hannah replied.

"Go away. I don't have any friends."

"If you're referring to those bullies that go around smashing mailboxes and shooting paintballs at people's garages, I would say you're lucky not to have any friends."

That got Pete's attention right away. He hurriedly looked up and studied Hannah with the most piercing blue eyes she had ever encountered. "Who told you about that?" Pete asked suspiciously.

"It doesn't matter. What does matter is I want to help you and keep you out of big trouble if you'll cooperate with me," Hannah answered.

"I don't know what you're talking about," Pete mumbled.

"Okay…well, I can just call the police right now, and we'll get to the bottom of this whole ordeal," Hannah announced with authority as she reached into her pocket and began pulling out her cell phone. Out of the corner of her eye, she saw the panic that suddenly began to consume Pete.

"W-wait, I don't want you to do that," Pete stammered.

"Are you going to talk to me and be honest? I don't have all day," Hannah stated in her matter-of-fact voice.

"It depends," Pete mumbled.

"On what?"

"I don't know…I can't think right now," Pete whined.

"Look, I think you are probably a nice guy that got mixed up with the wrong kind of guys. From what I can see, you don't act like you're having a good time. You look pretty miserable. Where are your so-called friends?"

"They're coming back," Pete answered.

"When?" Hannah asked.

"They didn't say for sure, but I have to give them my answer when they come."

"What answer? Come on, Pete, tell me what's going on so I can help you. It's obvious you're worried and don't want to do whatever they want you to do. I can help. The way I see it, you have two choices. You can be a part of their gang and end up in trouble and eventually go to jail, or you can join forces with me. We can nail them, and we can find you some good friends."

"I don't understand how you can help. You're just a lady."

"I'm not just any lady, and I have an incredible partner that you've already met," Hannah said with a smile.

"Who?" Pete asked curiously.

"You came to my door a few weeks ago and asked if my cat was a dog. Now do you remember?"

"No way! I knew that cat was something else. I told my gang about it, and they all teased me and called me a scaredy-cat, especially Dirk!"

"Well, how do you think Dirk's going to like having Harley tackle him and claw his back up if he doesn't cooperate?" Hannah asked.

"You know, I wouldn't mind seeing that," Pete said with a big smile on his face.

"Well, you may just get a front-row seat if you agree to help me, Pete. I have to know that I can trust you. Can I trust you, Pete?"

"Yeah, I guess."

"No, none of that 'I guess' stuff. It's either *yes* or *no*. What's it going to be?"

"*Yes*," Pete agreed.

For the next half hour, Hannah listened as Pete explained what the gang of boys were up to. She got a piece of paper and a pen out of her purse and wrote down Pete's phone number and address and the important particulars she had just learned from him. "When can I meet with you again?"

"Tomorrow right after school," Pete replied.

"Why don't you come over to my house around half past five? We don't want to arouse any suspicion if the bullies were to see us together at the park. From now on, I want you to act as if you're in total agreement with all of their plans. I have written down my home phone number and my cell phone so you'll be able to communicate what their plans are to me. Harley and I will use that information to form a counterattack, and we'll be ready with our team to help you. Can you do this, Pete? Can I trust you?"

"Yes, I'll do it and you can trust me," Pete said with a confident smile.

"I believe I can trust you, Pete. Do you feel better now that you've talked things through and you know you have me and my team on your side?"

"Yeah, I feel a lot better. I'll feel even better when all of this is over and those guys are locked up and can't do anything to me."

"Well, I better go for now so I'm not here when they get back. If you notice, Pete, I didn't say friends, I said 'bullies' because real friends don't do this kind of stuff. I'll see you tomorrow at my house at half past five."

"Is your cat going to hurt me?" Pete asked nervously.

"Only if you're not being straight with me. That's one incredible thing about working with animals: they can see right through you. There's no fooling them. Never forget that, Pete. I'll see you tomorrow, and I'm counting on you to do the right thing."

Chapter 7

Hannah yawned as she started the closing procedures at work. She was happy it was Friday, but a little concerned with the fast-approaching weekend. She glanced at the clock on the wall, noting it was a few minutes before five o'clock. Her heart skipped a beat when she thought about her upcoming meeting with Pete. What if he didn't show up? *Come on, Hannah, think positive.* She didn't want to even contemplate what the consequences would be if Pete decided to betray her.

"Have a good weekend, Hannah," Mr. Brown called to her as he went out the door.

"You too, Mr. Brown," Hannah answered back. Taking one last look around the office to make sure she hadn't forgotten anything, she turned off the lights and locked the door on her way out.

It didn't take long to get home, and she was relieved she had about fifteen minutes to spare.

"Meow…meow."

"Hello to you too, Harley. Are you ready for our meeting with Pete?"

"Meow."

"Remember, Harley, Pete is afraid of you. Please don't growl at him unless something is seriously wrong, okay?"

"Meow…meow."

"I understand that you're not thrilled with our meeting, but at this point, we're desperate. If our neighbor, Art, had his way, we would have been fired from our detective job last week. Let's hope Pete can help us figure out how to catch these vandals."

"Meow."

The doorbell rang, and Hannah said, "Here we go, Harley. Please be on your best behavior."

"Hi, Pete. Come on in."

She noticed that when Pete stepped inside the house, he was very apprehensive and kept cautiously looking around to see where Harley was. "Come into the kitchen, Pete, where we can sit at the table." Harley was waiting in the kitchen area, and Hannah noticed that he continually whipped his tail back and forth. "Pete, you remember my cat, Harley."

Both Pete and Harley stopped immediately in their tracks and took time to size each other up.

"H-hello, Harley," Pete managed to stammer.

"Meow," Harley responded.

"Wow, did he just talk to me?" Pete asked, surprised.

"Yes, he did. He said welcome, and he's looking forward to working with you," Hannah replied encouragingly.

"I've never really tried to talk to a cat before," Pete managed to say.

"Harley is an incredible cat!"

"Meow…meow."

"See what I mean? Even he agrees." Hannah laughed. "Well, come and sit down so we can figure out what we need to do. How did your meeting go with the bullies?"

"The good news is they don't suspect that I'm turning on them. If they did, I would already be dead by now."

"Well, we certainly don't want that now, do we? Do they have any upcoming plans for this neighborhood?"

"As a matter of fact, tomorrow night, or I should say early Sunday around two in the morning, they are planning on driving by, and any cars that are parked on the street or in driveways will get their windows shot out with a BB gun. A few days after that, they plan to leave notes in the mailboxes requesting money to be paid if people don't want a repeat of what happened."

"Wow, they don't mess around, do they?"

"No, they don't, and I don't want to be a part of it anymore. Someone could get hurt, and it's not fun seeing all the damage and knowing that I'm partly responsible."

"Getting a job and earning money the right way is definitely a better way to go," Hannah replied. "Did they give you a specific assignment?"

"Yeah, I'm supposed to be one of the lookouts and let them know if the police or anyone else is coming."

"Did you remember to bring the list of everyone's name, address, and phone number that are a part of this group of vandals?" Hannah asked.

Pete dug into his pocket and pulled out a paper. "I have everyone's name and some of their cell numbers and addresses. I'm sorry I don't have all the information you asked for, but it would look pretty suspicious if all of a sudden I started asking for their addresses and phone numbers."

"I understand. I'm glad you were able to get what you could. Based on what you've told me, here's what I think we need to do."

For the next hour, Hannah reviewed with Pete her plan of action. "There will be three cats, a Saint Bernard, and two horses that may be involved in the sting and takedown operation. I will also notify the police to see if I can get them involved when things start happening."

Pete got up from the table and slowly began walking to the door. "All I can say is I sure hope all of this works…because if it doesn't, I think everyone will know who the weak link is."

"I know it's easy for me to say 'don't worry, it's all going to be okay,' but my team will have your back, and we'll be there to help you all the way. The most important thing for you to remember, Pete, is you're not in this alone. Harley and I are in it all the way with you, and I don't want anything to happen to any of us. If anything does come up before tomorrow that you think I should know about, please don't hesitate to give me a call."

"Okay," Pete mumbled and then slowly pushed the door open to leave.

"Remember, you'll probably see Harley before you see me early Sunday morning when this whole thing starts to play out. Since he knows you now, I will have him cover you, and the other animals will watch the rest of the bullies," Hannah tried to reassure him.

Hannah closed the door and turned to Harley, asking, "Well, what did you think of our meeting?"

"Meow…meow."

"I agree. It sounds like we're not going to get much sleep Saturday night going into Sunday morning. We both might need a good nap tomorrow afternoon. Either way, Harley, I need you to alert Fluffy, Copper, Rocky, and the horses about what's going to be going down early Sunday morning and that we're going to need all of their help. Tomorrow morning, I will go to the police station and see if we can't get a couple of deputies to assist us. Once I know who's going to help, I'll let you know so you can give the other animals an update. All I can say is we have our work cut out for us. Let's go eat and then I think I'll go to bed. How about you, Harley?"

"Meow."

"I thought you'd want to go to bed early tonight."

Chapter 8

Hannah had just finished meeting with the police and was feeling relieved and grateful that there would be two policemen dressed in plain clothes that would be assisting her in the takedown of the gang of vandals. They were fully aware of the current vandalism situation and were pleased to learn that one of the gang members was willing to work with them to help break up the gang's activities. The only drawback was the police didn't want her and her little team to be involved; however, in the end conceded that if it weren't for her, they wouldn't have had any idea about what was going to happen early Sunday morning. She also clinched the deal when she advised that Pete might not cooperate if she wasn't there to help with the takedown plan.

Hannah yawned again for the umpteenth time and wondered how many more times she would keep yawning on her drive home. She didn't sleep well the night before because she couldn't stop worrying and plotting how her little team was going to bring down the bullies. She hoped Harley had been able to meet with his group of comrades, and once he briefed her on it, they could both go and take a good nap before the night's plan was put into action.

He was waiting at the door for her when she came in. "How's it going, Harley dog?"

"Meow…meow."

"I am sooo relieved! Thanks for the good news, Harley. I don't think I could have taken it if you had bad news. So your team is ready for tonight and everything's a go?"

"Meow."

"Well, how about a treat? And then let's go take a nap."

"Meow!"

Harley joined Hannah on her bed, and before laying down, she set the alarm so they would have plenty of time to get everything ready for the big sting later that night.

* * * * *

"Meow…meow."

Hannah came awake with a start and couldn't believe the alarm was going and Harley was meowing in unison at her. "Okay, okay… I'm awake."

"Meow!"

"I'm sorry, Harley. You're right I was in a deep sleep, and it's a good thing you and the alarm clock were making noise because I probably wouldn't have woken up."

"Meow…meow."

She swung her legs over the side of the bed and ran her fingers through her hair while she mentally began pulling her thoughts together. "I'm going to hurry and get dressed and then we can go downstairs and get a quick bite to eat."

"Meow."

Hannah was busy pulling on dark pants, shoes, and a matching sweatshirt when she glanced at the clock. It was 12:30 a.m., and the drive-by BB shootings were supposed to start around two in the morning. She was ahead of schedule, and that was a good thing. After tying her shoes, she hurried down to the kitchen, where Harley was waiting for her. "How are you doing, Harley?"

"Meow…meow."

"I'm a little anxious too. This is our first big case, and we need to do well so we can get more jobs after this one, right?"

"Meow."

Hannah reached into his treat bag and dropped several morsels into his bowl. As she watched him gobble them down, she smiled, thinking that there was nothing anxious or sluggish about his appetite. Next, she opened a can of chicken liver pâté and spooned it into his bowl, where he promptly began devouring his main course.

Hannah grabbed a cherry yogurt for herself and while eating, went through a mental checklist of everything she needed to remember.

"Meow."

"Are you ready to put our plan into action, Harley?"

"Meow...meow."

"Good kitty. Now you remember to be careful and remind the others to do the same. The bullies will have BB guns tonight, and we don't want anyone hurt. Harley, don't forget to be very protective of Pete."

"Meow."

She watched as Harley slid through his kitty door and ran down the back stairs to the yard. Walking over to the window, she saw Rocky, the Saint Bernard, Fluffy, and Copper waiting on the grass for him. Harley walked up to each animal, and they touched noses while he briefly communicated with each one. She watched in amazement and wished she could understand what was being said. And then they were off. The cats ran to the fence and easily jumped to the top railing and flew over. Rocky, weighing over two hundred pounds, strode powerfully to the side yard, where she had left the gate open for his easy access. She noticed that he had a long string of drool hanging from his mouth, and she couldn't help chuckling when he shook his head flinging the drool in all directions. *Good thing Harley didn't see you do that, Rocky! Be sure to save some of that for our bullies tonight!*

Hannah quickly walked over to the kitchen drawer by the refrigerator and reached inside to retrieve her flashlight and a small can of pepper spray, which she placed in the pockets of her sweatshirt. Next, she opened the pantry door and reached for the spare house key she kept for emergencies and then turned out the lights, walking cautiously to the front door. After opening the door, she shut it quietly and locked it, placing the key into the coin pocket of her pants. She stepped down the stairs of her front porch and rushed to hide behind the tall juniper tree in the corner of her yard. She carefully reached into her sweatshirt pocket and pulled the flashlight out to check the time. It was 1:15 a.m.

While her eyes adjusted to the darkness, she checked her surroundings for any sign of Pete or the two policemen. She glanced to the north in order to survey how many cars had been left out on the street or in driveways. She was surprised to see that many of her neighbors didn't park their cars in their garages. It was a good thing they were going to stop these bullies tonight or there'd be a lot of angry neighbors in the morning.

Hannah heard movement to her left, and when she looked down the street, she saw Pete running in her direction. Her first inclination was to call out to him, but thought better of it in case anyone else in his gang was watching. Just as she was about to call out to him, the silence was broken by a voice saying, "Hey, Petey, I'm surprised your mommy let you out this late at night," followed by a nasty laugh.

"I don't answer to you, Dirk, and I don't appreciate your rude comments," Pete growled back.

"Ohhhh, did I hurt your wittle feelings?"

"Hey, you two, shut up! What's the matter with you guys? Are you trying to wake up the whole neighborhood before we even get started?" Bill demanded.

Hannah watched and listened from a few feet away camouflaged by her large juniper tree. Her heart raced furiously while she thanked her lucky stars that she didn't blow her cover when she almost called out to Pete. Taking a deep silent breath, she leaned into the tree in order to try to catch every word of their conversation.

Fortunately, she had caught the majority of the instructions, enough to be able to anticipate most of their moves. She was extremely relieved when Bill instructed Pete to stay where he was and guard that end of the street while he and Dirk began walking northward to the other end to check on a guy named Craig. She didn't catch the name of the boy who would be driving the getaway car, but did hear that Dirk would be using the BB gun that would be shooting out the car windows.

"Meow."

"Hi, Harley. Is everyone in place on your end?"

"Meow."

"Here's what's going to happen. The getaway car is going to drive north on our street, pick up a boy named Dirk, flip a U-turn at the end of our street, and then speed back down our street, making one last U-turn. On its way back, Dirk will begin shooting, and when they reach the end of the street, they'll pick up the rest of the guys. Harley, I need you to go right now and talk to the horses and see if they can unlatch their big gate and push it open into the street, blocking the car so it can't get down the street to do any damage after they make their last U-turn. Let the other animals know that the rest of the gang will try to run for it when they see they're blocked in, and we'll need them to tackle and hold these guys down so the police can make their arrests. Can you do this, Harley?"

"Meow…meow."

"Fantastic! You're the best, Harley!"

"Meow."

She watched as Harley slipped quietly and quickly away. After checking her surroundings to make sure it was safe, she called out to Pete to let him know she was there.

"I'm relieved you're here, Hannah. Did you hear that idiot, Dirk? I sure would like to punch him," Pete said in frustration.

"I need you to stay cool and calm, Pete. Don't worry about Dirk. He's going to get his, I promise." They were interrupted by the sound of two men who were approaching them and looked like they were out for a walk.

"Oh great, now what are we going to do?" Pete asked with concern.

"Don't worry, I think it's our two policemen. They didn't wear uniforms in order to stay undercover."

"Hannah, are you here?" one of the men whispered.

"Yes. I'm behind the juniper tree. The young man on the south end of the tree is Pete."

"Pete, I am Officer Grant, and this is my partner, Officer Sheldon. We appreciate your stepping up to the plate and helping us bust these vandals. We'll talk more later, but for now, Hannah, bring us up to speed on what's going down."

* * * * *

"It sounds like you've got everything covered," Officer Grant said. "We'll both stay in the shadows so no one sees us. I'm going to go over and make sure the horses can get that gate open, and Officer Sheldon will move down to the north end so no one slips away when everything starts going down."

"You'll see my big cat named Harley. He's talking to the horses right now and will let the other animals know what's going on. If you see him, let him know that I sent you."

Hannah could see Pete fidgeting and said, "Okay, Pete, try to stay calm."

"Easier said than done," Pete replied nervously.

Hannah understood Pete better than he realized. She continually took in slow breaths, exhaling deeply to try to keep herself calm as well. Straining her ears to listen for anything unusual, she suddenly heard Pete say, "Show time. I can see Randy's car approaching now."

Hannah could feel her heartbeat racing off the charts and her adrenaline skyrocketing. *Please keep Harley and the animals safe, dear Father,* she whispered her prayer over and over as she readied herself for the situation ahead.

When the car drove by her hiding spot, she looked around the juniper tree in order to watch every movement firsthand. She didn't see Dirk get into the car when it reached the end of the street, but she did hear him slam the door after getting in. The getaway car was now making its first U-turn and starting its approach down to the end of the street where she and Pete were waiting. In anticipation of its arrival, she moved to the other side of the tree so she could see the final U-turn. Upon glimpsing the car, she could see Dirk rolling down his car window and watched as he positioned the BB gun in preparation for the night's activity. "Watch out, Petey, I might shoot you with my BB gun," Dirk called out, followed by his disgusting laugh.

The getaway car was now moving forward, and BB shots began to ring out in the silent night, along with the sounds of shattering glass as several cars got their windows shot out. Hannah sighed with relief when she saw the enormous gate swing out and instantly collide with the car, causing a loud boom that interrupted the shooting.

It was clear that the driver of the getaway car was shocked by the gate suddenly appearing out of nowhere, and soon the pandemonium exploded in full force. Within seconds, two large horses appeared and began rearing up at the car. Stunned by the aggressiveness of the horses, the boys were caught off guard and didn't see Officer Grant race around the back of their car with his gun pulled.

Yanking the door open, he demanded, "Drop your weapons and get out of the car now!"

The driver cooperated; however, as soon as Dirk got out of the car, he threw his BB gun at the officer, knocking him temporarily off balance, while he began to run away. Within seconds of Dirk's escape, a large Saint Bernard intercepted his flight by coming out of nowhere, tripping and tackling him. Along with being surprised by the attack, Dirk got the wind knocked out of him when he and Rocky hit the ground. If that wasn't bad enough, the biggest cat he ever saw in his life came up and swatted him across the face, leaving him with several painful bleeding scratches.

"Ouch! What the—This can't be happening!" Dirk whined. He stared as the cat touched noses with the Saint Bernard, and then he suddenly got very nauseated when the Saint Bernard dropped a huge ball of slime in his face.

Bill and Craig were at the north end of the street, staring in disbelief at what was taking place. Craig, having seen enough, yelled, "I'm outta here, man" and took off at a run.

Bill turned in time to see two cats fly through the air and attach themselves to Craig's retreating back, followed by what sounded like the worst cat fight he'd ever heard. He wasn't sure if it was Craig screaming or the cats, but before he could do anything about it,

Officer Sheldon handcuffed him and was walking him to a police car that had just pulled up.

Within seconds, two more police cars arrived on the scene, and it wasn't long before all the juveniles, with the exception of Pete, were handcuffed and sitting inside the police cars. Officer Grant had instructed Pete to get behind the juniper tree so the other juveniles wouldn't realize he had been in on the sting.

Once things were under control and there wasn't a threat to Hannah, she quickly began scouring the neighborhood to make sure Harley and his team were okay. To her huge relief and delight, all were accounted for and safe.

"Harley, I'm so happy everyone is safe. Wow, what a team we have! Everyone was incredible, and things couldn't have gone better!"

"Meow…meow!"

"I agree! We couldn't ask for a better team. Let everyone know we'll be handing out treats tomorrow afternoon for a job well done!" Hannah replied, relieved.

"Meow."

She watched in awe as Harley rounded up his team and they followed him back to their backyard.

"Hannah, congratulations on your amazing plan and team! I have to admit I've never seen anything quite like it!" Officer Grant said with a chuckle. "You definitely have a way with animals."

"Thank you, Officer Grant. I have to admit, they're one heck of a team! I'm also grateful that you and Officer Sheldon were here to help us. We never could have wrapped things up without your help."

"Well, that's what we're here for," Officer Grant replied. "We need to get this gang down to police headquarters and get them booked. We'll want to get in touch with you in the next day or so to get a statement from you and have you sign some forms. Will you be able to stop by the station?"

"Of course. I do have a couple of questions for you, Officer Grant. I'm sure the other boys are going to be asking about Pete. What will you tell them?" Hannah asked with concern.

"We will be as vague as possible so we don't let them know about his involvement. We don't want them to retaliate against him," Officer Grant answered.

"The boy I'm worried about most is Dirk, the one who did the shooting. For some reason, he really has it in for Pete. For a moment, I thought he was going to take a shot at Pete before he started shooting the cars."

"I'm glad you brought that to my attention. I will let the others know about your concerns at the station, and we will keep a close eye on Dirk. He is the one that will get the harshest sentence due to his using a weapon and going against an officer's instructions during the takedown."

"Well, I'm glad it's over and happy it turned out the way it did," Hannah replied.

"Your neighbors are pretty lucky to have someone like you in their neighborhood organizing a sting like you just did. Would you like a job on the force?"

"I think I'm going to have to pass on that. If any of my neighbors do ask about tonight, I would appreciate your informing them that I was the one who organized the sting to bring this gang down. They actually offered to pay me if I could figure out who was doing all the vandalism in our neighborhood and assist with bringing them in. I'm doing this to help supplement my income."

"I'll be happy to do that, Hannah."

"Also, there were several cars that got their windows shot out, and the neighbors that own the horses will probably have to get a new gate for their horse corral. They'll need to know how to handle that. Can you give me the information on what I should tell them?"

"There will be a case number assigned to this police incident," Office Grant advised Hannah. "Advise anyone that has suffered damage as a result to get the case number and turn that into their insurance. Do you by chance have the contact information on any of these juveniles?"

"Yes, Pete was able to supply some of the information. We do have all of their names, some phone and address numbers. He didn't want to arouse suspicion by asking them a day before all of this went down. I will bring the list with me when I come to the station tomorrow," Hannah replied.

"That sounds good. Thanks again for all your help, Hannah. I'm going to go now. I'm sure you must be tired. Go home and get some rest, and we'll see you tomorrow at the station."

Chapter 9

Hannah didn't get out of bed Sunday until noon. The events of the early morning seemed more like a nightmare now rather than reality. When she arrived downstairs in the kitchen, Harley was waiting for her.

"How are you doing today, Harley?"

"Meow."

"You're certainly doing better than I am."

"Meow…meow."

"I'm not sure I'm cut out for this detective stuff."

"Meow."

"I appreciate your vote of confidence, but I have to tell you, the verdict is still out for me. Let's have some breakfast, and maybe I'll start getting the pep back into my step."

"Meow…meow."

"I have to admit, I'm very impressed with you and your team, Harley! They were as good as any super heroes I've seen! Someday you will have to tell me your secret."

"Meow."

"You're kidding! You just bribe them with treats?"

"Meow!"

"Well, all I can say is, we better have some pretty amazing treats to give them."

"Meow…meow."

"Thank you for cluing me in on what they like so I can pick some up after I stop by the police station. They all definitely deserve them."

* * * * *

Hannah met with Officers Grant and Sheldon around two that afternoon. They made a copy of the list of names and pertinent information that was given to her by Pete. She had been informed that the juveniles were being cooperative, with the exception of Dirk, which didn't come as any surprise. Before leaving the station, she got a copy of the police incident report and case number so she would be able to assist those neighbors that might need help filing claims.

Remembering the treats that Harley had told her the animals preferred, she made a quick stop at the grocery store so they could keep their promise to the most important members of their detective team. She really couldn't have brought down these vandals without them!

"Harley, I'm home," Hannah announced when she came in.

"Meow."

"Don't worry, Harley, I stopped by and picked up everyone's treats. Let's get out some bowls, and we can get their treats ready."

"Meow."

Hannah liked to tease Harley, and she deliberately left his treats in the grocery bag while she filled the other bowls. When she finished, she asked, "How does that look, Harley?"

"Meow…meow?"

Hannah couldn't help chuckling and asked, "Did you need a treat too, Harley?"

"MEOW!"

"You know I wouldn't forget you, Harley dog!" Hannah teased as she hurried back to the pantry! She pulled out one more bowl and then reached inside the grocery bag to dump the remaining treats into the bowl. "How's that, Harley?"

"Meow...meow."

"You know I could never forget you, Harley! You're my partner!" She enjoyed carrying the treats outside to the awaiting Saint Bernard and cats, who were anxiously lined up in anticipation of their well-deserved rewards. "Thank you, Rocky, Fluffy, and Copper! You all did an incredible job! Enjoy your treats!"

"Meow."

"Don't worry, Harley, we'll take the horses their treats later on this evening. Everyone, eat up and thanks again for all of your help!"

* * * * *

Hannah heard the doorbell ring when she walked back into the kitchen and wondered who it could be.

"Hello, Hannah," Emily Ball greeted her after she opened the door. "I heard you had quite the night. If you're not too tired, I would love to come in so you can tell me what went on last night, or should I say this morning?"

Hannah briefly summed up what took place, leaving out Pete's name so it wouldn't get out which boy had stepped up to help bring down the gang.

"Congratulations, Hannah! I am so impressed with you and your team. I have to admit I wasn't sure if you could do it or not. This will sure shut Art up, won't it?"

"All I can say is, I'm happy his car wasn't one of the cars that got their windows shot out. I never would have heard the end of it!" Hannah said with a half chuckle.

"Well, I can tell you, you are certainly all the talk today. Even the police are talking about how amazing you are. And what's all this I hear about your using animals? I had no idea! Are you like an animal whisperer, Hannah?" Emily asked curiously.

"I can't tell all my secrets, Emily. Otherwise, I won't have a business left. The important thing is that I told you I would get the job done, and I did."

"You certainly did, Hannah. We are all looking forward to our neighborhood watch meeting on Wednesday, and I plan on passing around the jar for more donations, but we'll certainly pay you for a job well done."

"I appreciate it, Emily." Hannah walked Emily to the door and was thrilled to know she would be receiving an extra paycheck in a few days.

As Hannah got ready for bed that night, she was grateful that the Middletons, who owned the horses, were so understanding about their gate being damaged. Fortunately, the horses didn't suffer any injuries, and when she knocked on their door that evening bearing gifts for both them and their horses, they welcomed her into their home. They had an enjoyable visit, and she was able to give them more details about what had taken place, as well as provide them with an accident report to assist them with their insurance claim. She hoped her neighborhood watch meeting would go as well.

"Meow."

"I'm ready for bed. Are you, Harley?"

"Meow."

"I totally agree. I think this has been the longest day we've ever had! Let's call it a day, shall we?"

"Meow!"

Chapter 10

A few days later…Wednesday

"Did you hear about that lady who took down a gang of vandals in her neighborhood over the weekend with some cats, a Saint Bernard, and some horses?" Lance, one of the salesmen, asked.

"Yeah! Pretty incredible! Too bad they didn't say who she was on the news," Kyle replied. "I'd like to check her out!"

"It's my understanding she doesn't live too far away from our office," Brad added.

"Maybe Hannah knows her. Hey, Hannah, did you hear about that lady who took down a gang of vandals in her neighborhood over the weekend with some cats, horses, and a Saint Bernard?" Kyle asked.

"No, but I heard my neighbors talking about it," Hannah replied. "She sounds brave, crazy, or a little of both, doesn't she?"

Everyone had a good chuckle over that comment.

"Yeah," the group concurred.

Fortunately, the group conversation went on to another subject, and Hannah hoped she wouldn't regret later on not admitting her part in the whole ordeal. If Mr. Brown asked her about it, she would definitely tell him the truth and ask him not to reveal her part in it.

It was already Wednesday, and she still hadn't heard a word from Pete. She wondered if he was okay and thought it would be a good idea to call and check on him when she got home from work. Hopefully she would have enough time to squeeze in a call before leaving for her neighborhood watch meeting.

Harley greeted her at the kitchen door when she walked in for lunch. "How's the best detective kitty in the whole world today?" Hannah asked.

"Meow!"

"I agree! You are fantastic, Harley! Everyone is talking about you at the office, did you know that?"

"Meow...meow?"

"Oh, they just want to know who that incredible kitty is that helped take down a gang of vandals! If I'm not careful, pretty soon you're going to be famous, Harley. I hope you'll still talk to me. In fact, people will be lining up to get your paw-tograph!"

"Meow?"

"You want to know what a paw-tograph is? When people are famous, they're often asked for their autographs, which simply means they sign their name on a piece of paper. So now that you're famous, people will want you to give them a paw-tograph."

"Meow...meow."

"I have to agree with you, Harley! People are funny! Harley, have you or any of the animals seen Pete since everything went down?"

"Meow."

"That's what I'm concerned about. I thought I would have heard from him by now, and I'm worried about him. If it weren't a school day, I would call him right now. I hope he's okay."

"Meow."

"Thanks, Harley. Will you get the word out to be on the lookout for him? I hope I'm just overreacting."

"Meow."

Hannah checked the kitchen clock and said, "Looks like we have time to watch a little bit of *Judge JoJo*. Come on, Harley."

* * * * *

The afternoon at work seemed to drag by for Hannah. The phones were slow, which gave her a chance to catch up on the mountain of filing. It looked like no one had done any filing in several years, and she could understand why. All the completed files had been thrown in a heap in a back office, and the constant bending over and picking up to place them in a filing cabinet made her long for an afternoon nap.

She jumped a mile high when Mr. Brown asked, "How's it going, Hannah?"

"Sorry, Mr. Brown, you scared me. I didn't hear you coming. I'm doing okay. I can see why these files piled up. It isn't a very fun job trying to get things organized. It's a necessary job but not my favorite thing to do."

"Yes, it doesn't seem to be anybody's favorite thing to do. I appreciate you getting in here and working on it. I've been meaning to tell you, Hannah, I'm hearing lots of great compliments from our customers about our new receptionist who is very knowledgeable about our products, not like the last person we had answering the phones."

"Well, thank you, Mr. Brown. That makes me happy. I was going to tell you that I've been taking several brochures home and have been studying them so I would be able to answer customers' questions better. It's nice to know it's working!"

"It definitely is, Hannah, and thanks for taking the initiative to do that. I've been wanting to talk to you to see how you're enjoying your job. Is it a good fit for you?"

"I love the company and everyone here in the office. I am struggling to make ends meet on the salary I'm making, and I'm hoping something will come up where I could be transferred into a higher paying job," Hannah confided, hoping she wouldn't upset Mr. Brown by being honest.

She watched as Mr. Brown went over and closed the door. *Oh no, I should have kept my big mouth closed. Now I'm going to get fired,* Hannah worried.

"I'm closing the door, Hannah, because there is an opportunity that may be coming up in the near future that may be of interest, and it's still confidential. The company is working out the details with respect to income, etc., but I thought I would mention it to you and get your feedback on it," Mr. Brown replied.

Hannah sighed inwardly and leaned forward on the chair she was sitting on, eager to hear more about the job. "Yes, I'd love to hear more, Mr. Brown."

"Because we are a security systems company, we have received several requests for undercover agents to go in and do audits for large companies. Unfortunately, we do live in a world where people are tempted every day to make poor choices, and most companies prefer to hire an outside company to come in and investigate. Once an audit or investigation is completed, then the company's loss prevention or management team can come in and do the dismissing of the personnel based on our findings. Would you like to be considered for an undercover agent, Hannah?"

"I'd love to, Mr. Brown. In fact, I've been wanting to tell you about something I've been involved with. Did you catch the news about the lady that brought down a gang of vandals using a team of animals?"

"Yes, that was a fascinating news report," Mr. Brown stated with interest.

"Well, that lady was me. Several of the salesmen asked me earlier today if I knew anything about it, and I told them no. I told them no because I didn't want all the attention. I had planned to let you know it was me if the subject came up. I was at a neighborhood watch meeting about a month ago where a lot of neighbors informed the group that their homes had been vandalized and they were eager to hire someone. I volunteered to work without pay to prove to them that I could solve the case of who was doing the vandalism. We made an agreement that if I was able to bring down the gang, they would pay me. Tonight, we are having another homeowners' meeting. I will report back what I was able to do and they are going to pay me for capturing the vandals."

"Wow, Hannah, that is amazing! Sounds like this new position is right up your alley."

"It does sound promising, and I would love to know more about it when the details become available."

"Well, I'll let you get back to your filing. I'll keep you posted. Oh, and don't worry, I'll keep what you told me about bringing down the gang of vandals confidential."

"Thanks, Mr. Brown, I would really appreciate that."

Now that Hannah had something exciting to think about while filing, her afternoon flew by.

When she arrived home, she hurried to make dinner and after changing her clothes, realized there wasn't enough time to call and check on Pete and still be on time for the neighborhood watch meeting.

"Harley, I'm leaving for the neighborhood watch meeting now, and I'm excited about going because we should receive our first paycheck tonight."

"Meow!"

"I wish you could go with me, partner."

"Meow."

"You keep an eye on things here and I'll let you know all the details when I get back. Bye, Harley."

As she walked to Emily Ball's home, her mind raced through all the details of what happened on Sunday morning, causing her to wonder what would be best to share with her neighbors. She also carried the forms that the police department had given her for anyone who had suffered damage from the BB gun shooting. Before going up the steps to Emily's front door, she checked her watch and saw that she was about five minutes early.

"Welcome, Hannah! It's great to see you," Emily greeted her warmly, opening the door for her to enter. "Well, here's our guest of honor," Emily announced to the neighbors that had arrived early.

It didn't take long for them to begin asking questions, and at times, it became a little overwhelming. Hannah was grateful when Emily finally interrupted the interrogation and called the meeting to order.

"We definitely have a full house tonight, and I'd like to get started as I know all of you are anxious to hear the details of what happened the other night. Before turning the time over to Hannah, I want to pass the donation jar around again, and I hope everyone will give generously to show Hannah our appreciation for what she did to capture the gang of vandals that have been preying on our neighborhood."

Hannah marveled at the group's attention to her every word as she briefly related what had taken place. "I apologize to those neighbors who did suffer some damage, and I brought paperwork for you that can be submitted to your insurance for reimbursement. Lastly, there was one boy from the gang that didn't want to be involved in destroying anyone's property, and he fortunately assisted with the takedown of the other gang members."

"Well, just who is this boy?" Art demanded.

"He will remain nameless as we don't want to alert the other gang members that he was involved in stopping the vandalism," Hannah advised. "I am worried about him and would like to get him involved in some good activities where he can make some better friends. If any of you have some recommendations that I could relay to him and his parents, I would appreciate it."

"Let's give Hannah a big hand and show her our appreciation," Emily said as she carried over the donation jar and handed it to Hannah.

"Thank you, everyone. Please keep me and my detective company in mind if a situation should come up and you need an incredible team to help you."

Several neighbors came up to Hannah after the meeting and handed her a slip of paper with names of groups that they thought would help Pete. She planned to check into them to ensure that they would be a good fit for him.

She said her goodbyes and hurried home to Harley where she could show him their earnings and count the money they had earned together.

"I'm home, Harley."

"Meow."

"Look what I have, Harley dog!"

"Meow?"

"It's a jar of money. Money is what we need to buy your treats and pay our bills."

"Meow!"

Hannah chuckled and said, "Now you're impressed and I have your attention!"

With Harley supervising her, she dumped the money out on the counter and spent the next twenty minutes counting the money. "Wow, Harley, our neighbors were so generous. We made five hundred two dollars! That will sure help us until we can get our next job. I'm very happy and grateful."

"Meow...meow!"

"That goes double for you too! Thanks, Harley, for being the best partner I could ask for."

"Meow."

"Let's call it a day, shall we? Oh, and before I forget to ask you, have any of the animals seen any sign of Pete?"

"Meow."

"I was afraid of that. I'm really starting to worry about him. For sure, tomorrow, I have got to call and check on him. Don't let me forget...okay, Harley?"

"Meow."

"I'll race you upstairs!"

Hannah couldn't help laughing when she saw Harley whizz upstairs like a bolt of lightning! What she wouldn't give to be able to move like that!

Chapter 11

Hannah was wrapping things up at work on Friday afternoon and was looking forward to a quiet weekend. She thought about the previous weekend and the takedown of the vandals and was relieved that the weekend ahead would be much quieter.

Thoughts of Pete came to mind, and she hoped he was doing well. She had placed a call to him yesterday and had had a long talk with his mother. They had decided to send him to her sister's home for the rest of the school year where he would be surrounded with good cousins, and hopefully with the passage of time, things would settle down and when he returned home, he could start a more peaceful and productive life. She decided to keep the references she had received from her neighbors and would offer them to Pete's mother upon his return.

The doorbell rang, interrupting her thoughts. Harley followed her to the door, and when she answered it, she was greeted by several boy scouts. "We are having a food drive and will be by tomorrow morning to pick up your bag if you want to donate. Just leave your bag outside your door and we'll pick it up."

"Okay, boys, thank you," she stated as she reached for the bag while closing the door.

"Meow."

"I guess it's that time of the year, Harley. The holidays are just around the corner, and it's time to think of others." She walked back to the kitchen and opened the pantry door. "Let's see what we can give. How about some of this kitty food? What do you think, Harley?"

"Meow?"

Hannah couldn't help but chuckle at Harley's reaction to giving away some of his cat food. "I'm sure there must be a lot of hungry cats out there, just like there are hungry people."

"Meow…meow."

"That's a good kitty. Don't worry, I won't let you go hungry." He watched her as she placed a can of cat food in the bag along with several cans of beef stew, chili, and a variety of canned fruit. She tied a knot in the bag and said, "There, that should help a little," and walked the bag to the door so she'd be ready to put it on her doorstep the next day for pickup.

* * * * *

January 2000

The holidays had come and gone, and Hannah was relieved she survived financially through them. She hadn't heard any more about the job opportunity Mr. Brown had told her about previously, so in order to make ends meet, she had taken on a part-time job in retail sales during the holidays. She was sad that she had to pass on an invitation to spend Christmas with her children in California; however, with her tight budget, she barely had enough to buy presents for them, and airline tickets were totally out of the question. It was fortunate that they accepted her explanation of having to work her Christmas job. There was no way she was going to burden them by telling them just how tight things were for her.

The month of January was cold and snowy, and business at Security Systems had slowed down considerably after the holidays. Hannah's heart skipped a beat when Mr. Brown asked to meet with her just before lunch. While walking to his office, she wondered if she was going to be terminated due to the slowdown of business.

"How were your holidays, Hannah?" Mr. Brown asked after closing his office door.

"They were good. How were yours?" Hannah asked cautiously.

"Mine were good as well. I asked you to come in today because I have finally received some information from our home office on an undercover agent job that I thought you might be interested in."

"Oh yes, I would love to hear about it," Hannah responded with a sigh of relief.

"Are you aware of the craft store, Ruby's?" Mr. Brown asked.

"Yes, I have shopped there a couple of times."

"Well, it seems that they are experiencing cash shortages, and they suspect that the money is disappearing when it comes to their return procedures. They would like someone to go in, purchase an item, and then return it a few days later. They thought it would be beneficial to bring in someone that the employees don't know who could be an outside observer. Apparently, they suspect that some fraudulent returns are occurring with large amounts of money coming out of the cash registers, and they want to come up with a better procedure to see if this is what's happening. You would be there to review their current return process and would hopefully be able to observe and/or come up with a way to ensure that everything's on the up and up. What do you think?"

"I would love to be involved, Mr. Brown. As you're aware, I worked in retail many years prior to my coming here. When would I start?"

"I'll let management know you are willing to go undercover, and they'll let me know when they want you to start."

"Thank you, Mr. Brown. While we're waiting to hear back, I'll be putting some ideas together."

"Sounds great, Hannah. I knew you'd be the right person for this assignment."

"Thanks again, Mr. Brown." Hannah left his office relieved, and her mind was already at work on several ideas of return policies that she had used in her retail days and couldn't wait to take her lunch hour to go home and share the news with Harley.

* * * * *

"Isn't that great news, Harley?"

"Meow!"

"Now that the holidays are over and I'm not working my part-time job, I was beginning to worry about how we were going to make extra money. I hope they send me on this assignment soon so we can keep ahead of our bills."

"Meow…meow?"

"Good question, Harley. I think for right now, I'll be the only one handling this new assignment. I wish I could take you into the store, but I don't think they allow super cats like you."

"Meow."

"Don't worry, I still need you to keep a watch on our neighborhood. We don't want the vandalism to start up again. How's our team doing?"

"Meow…meow."

"I'm glad they're anxious for a new assignment. As soon as something comes up, we'll get everyone involved. For now, let's go watch some *Judge JoJo*."

Several days had come and gone, and finally Mr. Brown, upon his return from lunch on Thursday, asked Hannah to join him in his office.

"Management has received authorization from Ruby's for you to start your undercover job on Monday evening. Will that work for your schedule, Hannah?"

"Yes, I will make it work," Hannah replied positively.

"They are open until nine at night so you should have plenty of time after your workday here to go in and make your initial purchase. Be sure to keep a copy of your receipt so we can reimburse you for all of your expenses. Keep track of your mileage and time you spend on the job at Ruby's so we can reimburse those expenses as well. Ruby's has stated that they will pay a flat fee of two hundred-fifty dollars for your first observation, plus any expenses incurred by you. Does that sound agreeable to you, Hannah?"

"Yes, Mr. Brown. Do I report my observations to you, or will there be a contact person from Ruby's that I should talk to?"

"Ruby's wanted to make sure that you're in agreement with their proposal and then they will inform us of their loss prevention agent, and you will communicate your findings to that individual. Of course, if you do have any questions or concerns, you are more than welcome to talk to me at any time."

"Thank you, Mr. Brown.

Monday evening finally arrived, and Hannah was anxious to begin her new assignment at Ruby's. It had been over a year since the last time she had shopped at Ruby's, and she looked forward to going shopping. Even though it was January, the stores were always a season ahead with their displays. Everywhere she looked, she could see spring displays, and it made her excited for the warmer weather.

She enjoyed walking up and down the aisles of spring décor, noticing all the artificial spring flowers and bushes. She especially liked seeing her favorites of daffodils and tulips and little bushes of pansies. Everywhere she looked, she was surrounded by a spring wonderland.

Her next stop took her down the aisle that contained displays of every kind of Easter basket imaginable. From pinks, lavenders, yellows, and turquoise colors, there were assortments of bunnies and chicks to go with them. After only a few minutes in the store, she remembered why she had to stay away. Everything she looked at was irresistible, and the temptation to spend money was overwhelming.

Okay, Hannah, get a hold of yourself and remember why you're here! Taking a deep breath, she picked up a turquoise basket and a cute white bunny to go inside and placed them in her shopping cart. On her way to the cash and wrap area, she made a quick detour back to the aisle with the flowers and grabbed one of the pansy bushes. She knew she was getting too attached to the turquoise basket and bunny and wouldn't be able to return them, but was pretty sure she could convince herself to return the pansies in a few days. She promised herself not to look at anything else and headed straight to the checkout area to pay for her items. While standing in line, she smiled inwardly, thinking how difficult this assignment was becoming.

Deciding to put on her undercover agent hat, she began to pay attention to her surroundings and started by observing what the employees were doing around her and if there were any returns in process. She could see an employee pushing a cart around with a variety of items in it. As she continued to study her, she realized she was putting inventory back where it belonged. Another employee was marking items with a price gun, and it wasn't busy enough at the registers for anyone to do a return. As far as she could tell, nothing seemed amiss, and soon she had paid for her items and was on her way out to the parking lot. She did notice the name tags of several of the employees she observed and once in her car, got out her notebook and wrote notes about those she had observed and what they were doing along with the time she had observed them. She finished her entry by dating the page and including the amount of time she had spent at the store. When she got home, she would add her mileage to and from Ruby's.

The following morning, Mr. Brown stopped by her desk on his way into the office and asked if she was able to go shopping at Ruby's. She responded that all had gone well and she planned to return Wednesday evening after work to return one of her items. She also showed him the copy she had made of her receipt, and he gave her the thumbs-up sign, looking very pleased with her progress.

When Hannah walked into Ruby's Wednesday evening, there were several people in line, and the store seemed busier than it had been on Monday.

"Good evening. How can I assist you?" the Ruby's employee named Mandy asked Hannah.

"I have a return," Hannah replied.

"I need you to fill out this paperwork and then I will take care of your return," Mandy stated.

Hannah completed the form, which included her address and phone number and handed it back to Mandy. She watched as Mandy quickly did the return and handed her back the change for the pansy bush. Everything seemed to be in order; however, as Hannah walked away from the customer service desk, she noticed that Mandy began entering another transaction into the register, and there wasn't another customer in line behind her. She wished she could see what she was doing and mentally noted the time of day so she could talk to Ruby's loss prevention agent about what she had just observed.

She heard the cash register drawer open and turned in time to see Mandy pulling out some money. She tried not to be obvious about watching her, but was definitely curious about what Mandy could be up to. Slipping behind a floral display, she could still see Mandy and noticed immediately that she had placed a few bills into her apron pocket. She also saw Mandy looking around the area to ensure that no one was watching her. Hannah did a disappearing act as soon as she could, hoping not to draw any attention to herself. After a few minutes had elapsed, Hannah walked as nonchalantly out the front door of the store to the parking lot as quickly as possible while her heartbeat began to increase and her adrenaline kicked into high gear.

Once inside her car, she grabbed her notebook and began entering the events of the evening. It was a shame that she didn't have the name of the loss prevention contact because the urge to share her findings with someone were overpowering. She could only hope that tomorrow would come fast and that Mr. Brown would have a contact she could get in touch with.

Chapter 12

Hannah was up early the next morning, and Harley could tell from her body language that something was certainly up.

"Meow…meow?"

"You're right, Harley, I am upset and preoccupied with something. It's from this new case I'm on. I witnessed someone stealing money from the cash register last night, and that's never a good thing."

"Meow!"

"I need to report it to someone, and Mr. Brown hasn't given me a contact to talk to yet. I'm anxious to get to work today to discuss it with him, and that's why I'm up earlier than usual."

"Meow…meow."

"I wish you could help me on this case, Harley. I miss having your help."

"Meow."

"I plan on talking to Mr. Brown as soon as he arrives, and hopefully he can call Ruby's and get me the name of the loss prevention agent."

Hannah must have checked the clock on the wall at work a thousand times and was just about ready to give up on seeing Mr. Brown when she finally glimpsed his car pulling into the parking lot.

"Good morning, Mr. Brown. I need to talk to you as soon as possible about something very important, and it really can't wait," Hannah stated in an urgent tone.

"Come into my office right now and let's discuss what's on your mind," Mr. Brown replied.

It didn't take long for Hannah to relay the events of the previous evening, and she waited anxiously to hear his response to her news.

"Wow, Hannah, it sounds like you hit the tip of the iceberg. Nice job. Let me get Ruby's on the phone, and I will tell them it's imperative that I need the name of their loss prevention agent so you can give them the details of your discovery."

"Thank you, Mr. Brown. I'll go back to my desk and wait to hear from you," Hannah said, relieved.

Just before lunch, Mr. Brown called her back to his office and gave her the name of the loss prevention agent, Drew Williams, and his phone number.

"Okay, Drew, I need to hear from you soon. The sooner, the better," Hannah mumbled to herself while opening the door out to the parking lot. It was lunchtime, and as she walked to her car, she could still picture vividly the events of the previous night of seeing Mandy blatantly enter a transaction, the cash register drawer opening, and then witnessing her slip several bills into her apron pocket. The situation was certainly unfortunate and brought anguish and sorrow to her mind when she contemplated the consequences it would bring to Mandy once she was confronted with her actions. This was the difficult part of her role as an undercover agent. Sooner or later, the wrongdoer would be found out and would have to suffer for their choices.

"Meow?"

"Hi, Harley. Yes, I'm still gloomy."

"Meow?"

"I talked to Mr. Brown, and he gave me the name of the loss prevention agent. His name is Drew Williams, and I should hear back from him hopefully this afternoon."

"Meow."

"It's sad when people make bad decisions. Sooner or later, they always get caught and then they have to pay for their choices. I'm glad I learned when I was a little girl not to steal."

"Meow?"

"Yes, I stole a candy bar when I was about six or seven, and my mother caught me eating it. She took me back to the store, and I had to tell the store manager what I did. It was terrible! I thought I was going to have to go to jail."

"Meow?"

"No. Fortunately I didn't have to go, and I lost some fun privileges at home. I couldn't play outside with my friends or watch TV for a couple of days. My mother wanted to make sure I knew what it would be like if I had to go to jail. She even made me do extra chores around the house! Trust me, Harley, that was enough to make me not want to steal again."

"Meow!"

"You can say that again! Anyway, I feel sad that Mandy's going to have to learn the hard way. Let's have some lunch and watch *Judge JoJo* before I have to go back to work."

"Meow."

The phones were busy in the afternoon at work, and each time she answered them, she wondered if it would be Drew calling. She was going through her closing procedures when he finally did call.

"May I speak to Hannah North?"

"This is Hannah North."

"Hello, Hannah. This is Drew Williams with loss prevention at Ruby's. I understand from Mr. Brown that you made a discovery at one of our stores last night?"

"Yes, Mr. Williams, I did."

"Would you be able to meet with me this evening to review the details?"

"Yes. Where and when would you like to meet?" Hannah asked.

"Would you be able to meet me at Applebee's around seven? Let's plan on getting a bite to eat, and you can tell me everything at that time. Is that going to work for you?" Drew inquired.

"Yes, that will work fine."

Hannah hadn't been out to dinner with a man in several years and was a little nervous when she approached the front door of Applebee's. A large man dressed in khakis and a nice shirt opened the door from the inside and asked, "Are you Hannah North?"

"Yes, you must be Drew Williams."

He nodded his head and turned to let the host know Hannah had arrived, and they followed him to a table with a window view in the back of the restaurant where it was a little more secluded from the other guests. She slid shyly into the booth opposite him and accepted the menu the host gave her and waited nervously for Drew to take the lead.

"Have you ever eaten at Applebee's?" Drew asked.

"No, I haven't. Have you?"

"Yes. They have lots of great salads or chicken and meat dishes. My favorite item to order is the Oriental chicken salad. It's on the second page of the dinner menu. I recommend it or anything else that looks good," Drew responded while smiling at her over the top of his menu.

Hannah smiled back and thought how handsome Drew was. His hair was almost completely gray, with a few strands of his brown color competing here and there. He had large pale blue eyes and a friendly smile with straight white teeth that illuminated dimples in each cheek when he smiled. She was thrilled that he appeared to be more in her age range, and they would probably have more in common than someone who had just graduated from college and had just entered the workforce.

"I think the Oriental chicken salad sounds delicious," Hannah replied.

When their waiter arrived to take their order, they each ordered the salad and a soft drink.

"I understand you have been asked to be an undercover agent for Ruby's," Drew started the conversation again after the waiter left.

"Tell me, what happened last night when you were at one of the Ruby stores?" Drew questioned.

Hannah quickly brought him up-to-date on making a purchase on Monday evening and then explained the details about returning the pansy bush the previous night. All had seemed routine on the return until she had witnessed Mandy doing another transaction when she had left the register area without any customers present, opening the cash register, and then slipping several bills into her apron pocket. While waiting for his reaction and response, she grabbed her purse and pulled out the notebook she used to document her visits to Ruby's. "All of this occurred at seven thirty-eight in the evening on Wednesday."

"I'm glad you noted what time it was when you witnessed everything because it will help when we do our investigation," Drew said, impressed with her notebook details.

"I worked in retail for many years before switching to Security Systems, so I have had a lot of experience," Hannah replied humbly.

They were interrupted when the waiter brought their meal. The tantalizing smells of the freshly grilled chicken and vegetables made Hannah suddenly realize how hungry she was. They were each given a special sauce to drizzle over the salad, and Hannah couldn't wait to have her first bite.

Drew watched to see her reaction and wasn't disappointed when Hannah, without realizing it, smacked her lips in appreciation. "It looks like you're enjoying the Oriental chicken as much as I am," he said with satisfaction.

"Thank you so much for recommending it. It's every bit as good as you said it would be!"

Their dinner conversation flowed easily between them, and each took a turn sharing their work experience. Hannah felt relaxed and realized she hadn't enjoyed herself this much in a long time. In fact, she couldn't resist checking, as inconspicuously as possible, to see if he was wearing a wedding ring. When she didn't see one, she was secretly delighted and hoped he was enjoying her company as much as she was his.

"So, what happens now?" Hannah asked.

"Tomorrow I will visit the store and will make it appear as if it's just a routine visit. When I talk to the store manager, I will ask to see the tapes for the register and will pull the ones for Wednesday and will have a look at that night to review what happened around that time."

"I made a copy of my original receipt, and now that I think about it, Mandy didn't give me my original receipt back. I purchased three items and returned one item, the pansy bush."

"That's good to know. Do you by chance have the original transaction number on your receipt?" Drew inquired.

"Yes, and you're in luck. I have the copy in my purse. It is transaction number 9046."

"Good job, Hannah," Drew said as he noted the transaction number in a notebook he had brought into the restaurant. "This will really help me when I begin to track things down. I wish all of our undercover agents were as efficient as you," Drew said with a grin. He stared at Hannah and couldn't help thinking that maybe it was a good thing that all the undercover agents weren't like Hannah. He could stare at her strawberry-blonde hair and sapphire-blue eyes all night. Being in her company was refreshing and fun, and he was trying to think how he could prolong their evening together.

Hannah glanced at her watch and was shocked when she saw it was nine thirty already. "Oh dear, I didn't realize how late it was getting. I hope I haven't talked your ear off, Drew. Since my husband passed away and my children live in California, sometimes when I am in great company like yours, I tend to talk too much."

Drew, caught off guard by her comment that she was a widow, rushed to say, "No need to apologize. I have to admit I probably talked too much as well. I hope I don't sound forward by saying this, but I really enjoyed our time together tonight. My wife passed away a few years ago also, and it was nice to talk about business, and I enjoyed your company this evening. I would like to do this again, that is, if you would like that?"

"I would love to, Drew, and thanks."

The waiter had long ago left the bill for the dinner, and Drew picked it up and said, "I guess it's that time. Before we leave, would it be okay if I got your phone number?"

"Of course." She reached into her purse and tore a blank sheet of paper out of her notebook and wrote down her name and phone number. While she did that, she noticed him reaching into his wallet for an extra business card. They reached across the table, and their fingers touched while exchanging information. It felt wonderful to hold Drew's hand, even if only briefly, and then they stood to leave.

"Thanks again, Hannah, for agreeing to meet me. I will let you know how my investigation goes, and we can see where things take us. How does that sound?"

"Perfect," Hannah said with a smile.

They walked up to the front of the restaurant, and Hannah thanked him again for dinner and waved goodbye as Drew walked over to take care of the bill. She hadn't been this happy in a long time and almost wanted to skip to her car but thought better of it in case she should trip and fall.

*****

"Hello, Harley! How's my Harley dog?"

"Meow…meow…meow."

"I know it's late, Harley. I hope you didn't worry about me. I had the most wonderful evening. I met someone special."

"Meow?"

"Yes, I did go to my undercover meeting. I met with the loss prevention agent, Drew Williams, I was telling you about earlier. He was so nice and even handsome."

"Meow?"

"I know I sound a little crazy…but have you ever been in love, Harley?"

"MEOW!"

Hannah couldn't help the giggle that escaped her mouth at his reaction. "Well, if you must know, it is a wonderful feeling to be in love. Sometime when we have a lot more time, I'll tell you all about it." She tried to stifle a yawn, but it came anyway. "Let's go upstairs and get ready for bed. Morning will be here before we know. Come on, I'll race you!"

Chapter 13

Hannah was in an extra good mood the following day in spite of missing out on her normal eight hours of sleep, and she knew the reason was a new man in her life, Drew. Even the filing in the backroom couldn't get her down as she continued to hum and plow her way through the mountain of files. Each time the phone rang, her heart would jump into her throat when she imagined hearing Drew's voice on the other line. However, by the end of the day when he never called, she was feeling disappointed and wondered if she had imagined his feelings for her. She thought back on her days in retail management and tried to justify his not calling due to his work responsibilities in trying to resolve the loss prevention situation. There was one thing she was grateful for, and that was she wasn't the one that had to deal with Mandy and her consequences.

Harley was waiting for her at the door when she arrived home and welcomed her with a warm "meow."

"How's my Harley?"

"Meow…meow."

"I'm glad you had a good day. I was hoping to hear from my new friend, Drew. However, I guess he was too busy to call or he wasn't able to. He has a challenging job, and one never knows what can happen in those situations. I'm glad it's Friday and the weekend is here. I'm ready to relax and have some fun. How about you, Harley?"

"Meow."

"Let's make some dinner and find something good on TV, shall we?"

"Meow."

Hannah opened the refrigerator and saw her leftover Oriental chicken salad from Applebee's that she had brought home and her mouth began to water when she remembered how tasty it was. The only thing missing was the great company she had had the previous night, but she was determined to enjoy her Friday night anyway.

As she was getting the silverware out of a kitchen drawer, she remembered the Hawaiian rolls she had purchased earlier in the week and thought about how yummy they would be with her leftover salad. Once she had everything ready, she grabbed a TV tray and placed it in front of her television and channel surfed until she came to a station that was playing mystery movies.

She and Harley enjoyed getting thoroughly immersed in the plot of each mystery movie so they could test out their detective skills to see if they could solve the crime before the movie ended, revealing who had done it. Not to brag, but even she had to admit they were getting quite proficient at cracking these cases!

When the movie ended, she said to Harley, "We did it again, Harley! Another mystery solved by H & H Investigations! We really should go into business, you know?"

"Meow!"

"I know you've been telling me that for years! I'm glad I finally started listening to you!"

"MEOW!"

"Okay, okay, don't rub it in. I think I need to go to bed. How about you?"

"Meow."

* * * * *

The sun was just rising above the mountaintops, and several rays of sunshine were beginning to peek through the slits of the shutters in Hannah's bedroom. She could feel Harley stretching and heard him giving himself his morning bath. She didn't want to get up yet and tried to pretend that she was still sleeping.

"Meow."

"I guess Mr. Harley isn't buying my performance! Why do you have to wake up so early Harley? Can't a girl get any beauty sleep around here?"

"Meow."

"I guess not. Okay, give me a minute and I'll be down to start breakfast."

When she met Harley in the kitchen, she couldn't resist walking over to the kitchen window to admire the sunshine and the beautiful morning. The month of March had come in like a lion, with a few snowstorms, but was quickly mellowing into a lamb as spring was trying to desperately make its appearance known. She loved seeing the crocus plants popping up through the ground and the new buds emerging on the trees. It wouldn't be long until the buds opened up, along with the spring flowers, revealing the splendor of spring colors in a manner only Mother Nature could provide.

"Meow…meow."

"Hey you, you know how much I love flowers. Spring only comes once a year, and I don't want to miss anything."

"Meow."

"Apology accepted. Okay, let's get you your breakfast and a few treats and then I can go back to watching the spring flowers!"

Once Harley was contently eating his breakfast, Hannah grabbed a cherry yogurt from the refrigerator, along with a spoon, and stood at the window daydreaming about an award-winning backyard with every flower imaginable planted in the perfect setting, replacing every weed she saw instead. "Oh, wouldn't it be nice to be rich, Harley?"

"Meow?"

"Why? Because then we wouldn't have to work so hard or worry. We could come downstairs, and we would have servants cooking our breakfast…I could look out our kitchen window and see a glorious garden of flowers and not have to imagine it. We could have everything we want, and if something breaks down, like the washing machine or furnace, we don't have to worry about having enough money to fix it."

"Meow."

"You're right, Harley. I guess you don't understand about those things. You're already living the rich life in a way, aren't you? Don't get me wrong, Harley, I have a lot to be thankful for. Sometimes it's just nice to think about all the things you don't have and for a moment imagining that you do have them and how wonderful it would be. I'm sure there are problems whether you're rich or poor. I think that's why so many people try to win the lottery. Most of us will never win, but it's fun to imagine what life would be like if you did."

"Meow…meow."

"You're right, Harley! Time for me to quit daydreaming and get to work, or my whole Saturday will be gone and I'll wonder what happened to my weekend." On that thought, Hannah went upstairs and got dressed.

Saturday was typically spent in segments of cleaning, grocery shopping, working in the yard, and doing errands. As she was getting dressed and running a brush through her hair, she decided a visit to the hairdresser was certainly in order. If she had any hope of catching Drew's attention, she needed to look her best, and a hair trim was a good place to start.

The day flew by like she knew it would, and when she crawled into bed that night, the cool crisp sheets felt like heaven on her tired legs.

Sunday came and went as well, and Hannah was thinking about her workweek ahead when her thoughts were interrupted by the phone ringing. To her surprise and delight, Drew was on the phone, and they had a short but enjoyable chat. Before hanging up, she had agreed to meet him at the Olive Garden Monday evening at seven. He had told her he wanted to bring her up-to-date on the situation with Mandy, along with a few other items, which, of course, aroused her curiosity and made falling asleep that night challenging.

Hannah hurried to get ready for work the following morning and took extra pains with her hair, anticipating her meeting with Drew later that night. She took a final look in the mirror before heading out the door for work and was glad she had gone in for a haircut because she was having a great hair day.

Her fellow employees came in complaining and grumbling about it being Monday and that the weekend had gone way too fast; however, Hannah smiled inwardly thinking about seeing Drew that evening and couldn't be more happy that it was Monday!

Mr. Brown was curious about how her meeting with Drew Williams had gone the previous week and stopped by Hannah's desk so she could inform him on the latest details, along with the information that she had another meeting with him that night. "I hope all goes well, Hannah, and I'm sure he is pleased with everything you're doing. If anything comes up that you need my help with, please don't hesitate to let me know."

"Thanks, Mr. Brown. I appreciate all you have done for me, and I'm so grateful that you recommended me for this assignment."

The rest of her workday was spent watching the clock on the wall tick slowly by in between answering the phones and herding people to the various offices for their scheduled appointments. Finally, it was time to start her closing procedure and Hannah was anxious to complete it and be on her way. She took one last look at the clock on the wall and saw that she had enough time to stop home and check on Harley, as well as freshen up.

"Hello, Harley. How was your day?"

"Meow."

"Did you remember I have an appointment tonight with Drew?"

"Meow?"

"Yes, again. He wants to let me know how things went with Mandy. She's the girl that took the money out of the cash register, remember?"

"Meow."

"I have just enough time to get your dinner and a few treats and run upstairs to finish getting ready."

"Meow?"

"I'm not sure how late I will be. Drew said he had a few other things he wanted to talk to me about. I want you to keep an eye on things, and I'll be home as soon as I can."

"Meow."

Hannah checked her hair and added a few spritz of her favorite perfume, then headed downstairs. "See you later, Harley dog."

Harley loved his food and seemed to be concentrating on it rather than her leaving, causing Hannah to laugh while mumbling, "That's why you're such a big kitty. You love your food, and I love you!"

Hannah pulled into the parking lot at the Olive Garden within seconds of Drew, and she noticed he made his way over to her car to greet her.

"Hello, Hannah. It's good to see you again. How are things going?"

"I'm doing great, Drew, thanks for asking. I'm anxious to hear how things are going for you."

"Well, let's just say it's not one of those fun things I like to do but have to do in this case. Let's get a table, and I'll fill you in on all the details."

They only had to wait a few minutes for a table to become available and were soon seated at a booth, and it didn't take long to place their order. Drew looked across the table, admiring Hannah while thinking how nice it was to have someone to share dinner with, as well as unburden the pressures of his day. He could get used to having her around.

Hannah wondered what Drew was thinking and hoped he liked what he saw. She was about to say something when their waiter came with their salad, garlic sticks, and soft drinks. "You look lost in your thoughts, Drew. I hope everything went as well as possible."

"I'm sure you know from experience it's never enjoyable to have to confront someone who has made a poor choice. Needless to say, Mandy did finally own up to what she did and also enlightened us on a couple of other things that were going on that caused the store to have some significant shortages. Who knows how long this would have continued if we hadn't sent you in there, Hannah? We're pleased that you were able to catch her in the act and alert me to what was going on so quickly."

"I'm glad I could help," Hannah responded cheerfully.

"I spoke with Ruby's management team, and they would like to know if you'd be interested in coming up with a return procedure that would better safeguard or prevent a situation like this occurring in the future. They obviously need some help in keeping their losses down and are willing to pay you additional income to come up with something."

"I'll be happy to come up with some ideas. Is there a timeline that they need it by?" Hannah asked.

"They would love it yesterday, but will take it as soon as you can put it together," Drew said with a big grin on his face.

Hannah smiled back and felt pleased with another opportunity to increase her income. She was sure she and Harley could come up with some helpful ideas.

She was enjoying Drew's company and conversation, and the food was delicious as well. She wished the night could go on forever, but all good things have to come to an end. The waiter brought over a box for Hannah to place her leftover meal in and slipped the bill to Drew.

"Before we leave, I wanted to know if you'd like to go to a movie with me on Friday night, Hannah."

"Yes, I'd love to," Hannah responded happily.

"Do you have a preference on what we go and see?"

"To tell you the truth, it's been so long since I've gone to see a movie, I'm not even sure what's playing," Hannah admitted.

"Well, that's your next assignment," Drew said with a wink. "See what's playing, and when I call you later in the week, we can decide what we want to see."

Chapter 14

Hannah called out to Harley when she walked in the door on her lunch hour on Wednesday afternoon. "You must have been in the middle of a good nap when I called you," Hannah said with a chuckle. "I was beginning to worry about you, Harley dog."

"Meow."

"Are you tired today?"

"Meow…meow."

"Why are you worried about me?"

"Meow…meow."

"Oh…well, I can understand your concern about our writing some new policies for Ruby's and then my having to go in and audit their stores and possibly making some people mad. You know I'll be careful because I don't want anything bad to happen either."

"Meow."

"For now, let's get you some treats, and I need an apple and some nuts for lunch." Hannah kept an eye on Harley and noticed right away that he still wasn't acting as enthusiastic about things as he normally did, and she hoped he wasn't getting sick. She couldn't help wondering, what if there was something to worry about? Cats are supposed to be intuitive and have nine lives. Harley's intuition might know something that she didn't and she may need to watch her step. It was definitely something to be aware of and to keep in mind.

*****

Friday had arrived, and Hannah was looking forward to her date with Drew and was anxious to get the office closed so she would have enough time to go home and freshen up. The last appointment had just wrapped up, and she was able to start her closing process. It appeared that the whole office was anxious to begin their weekend, and she didn't have any trouble getting things put away and chasing people out of the office so she could lock the office door.

As she pulled into her garage, she thought about her date with Drew and the fact that he would be picking her up at her home. This would be the first time Drew would be meeting Harley, and she hoped that they would like each other. She checked the clock on her car's dashboard and decided it would be a good idea to remind Harley that Drew would be coming by to pick her up. Fortunately, he was waiting for her by the door when she came in.

"How's my Harley?"

"Meow."

"Did you remember I have a date with Drew tonight?"

"Meow?"

"Yes, he'll be here in about a half hour." She ran upstairs so she could change into some jeans and noticed that Harley wasn't far behind her. "I hope you like him, but if you don't, you can tell me honestly later tonight when I get home, okay?"

"Meow."

"Don't worry, I will leave your dinner out and some treats right after I finish changing my clothes." Hannah was glad she had washed her hair the night before and that it was still holding its style. She took one last look in the mirror and felt pleased with her appearance and then raced Harley downstairs. Of course, there was no contest. His four legs could beat her two legs any day of the week. She had just finished filling his bowl with food when the doorbell rang.

"Okay, Harley, that's probably Drew. Time to put on your best behavior."

"Meow."

"Hello, Drew, please come in," Hannah said as she opened the door to allow him to enter. She noticed that Harley was acting timid and was hiding behind her legs while nonchalantly peeking his head around to catch a glimpse of Drew.

"Well, hello there, BIG guy. I certainly have heard a lot about you, and I'm pleased to meet you," Drew said, extending his hand down to Harley to allow him to smell and assess it.

Harley seemed impressed with the compliment of "BIG guy" and decided he would come out and strut his stuff, showing off what a BIG kitty he was.

"Wow, Hannah, you weren't kidding about Harley. I think he's the biggest cat I've ever seen." Looking at Harley, he said, "No wonder your family calls you Harley dog! I think you and I are going to get along just fine, BIG guy."

"Meow."

"I think that was a definite yes from Harley," Hannah said with a smile on her face. "I was just getting out Harley's dinner, and he's due a few treats. Maybe you'd like to help with that, Drew."

"Absolutely, just point me in the right direction." All three went into the kitchen, and Drew reached into Harley's treat bag and gave him a generous helping.

"Okay, Harley, now that you're spoiled, Drew and I are going to be on our way. You watch the house, and I will see you in a few hours."

Harley paid no attention to Drew or Hannah, but instead continued to gobble down his treats. "He definitely knows his priorities," Drew said with a laugh while escorting Hannah to the front door.

They were soon on their way enjoying their drive in Drew's blue convertible Mustang. Hannah confessed that she always loved and wanted a Mustang and hadn't ridden in one since she was in her twenties. She was thrilled when he put the top down. It made her feel like a teenager as the wind whipped through her hair.

"I thought we'd pick up a couple of Philly steak sandwiches and eat them while we watch our movie. Are you okay with that, Hannah?"

"I would love that, Drew! This is turning out to be one of the best dates ever…riding in my favorite kind of car and eating my favorite food!"

The evening was everything she could have hoped for, and she hated to see it end. Drew was very attentive to her, and they appeared to enjoy the same things. They were never at a loss for words, and she felt totally at ease in his presence. She especially liked that he was a gentleman and insisted on opening doors for her. At the end of their date, he held her hand tenderly as he escorted her up to her front door. "I had a wonderful time with you, Hannah. Thank you for spending the evening with me."

"It was my pleasure, Drew. I don't remember the last time I had such an enjoyable evening." She watched him smile as he leaned down to take her lips in his. The kiss was tender and sweet, and it was breathtaking to experience such a warm closeness with someone again. They shared several kisses and ended their evening with a heartfelt hug.

"Good night, Hannah. I look forward to seeing you again soon."

"Good night, Drew."

After Hannah went inside, she checked to make sure the doors were locked and walked through the house to turn off the lights. When she went upstairs, she smiled at finding Harley already asleep on the bed.

"Good night, Harley."

* * * * *

Hannah had an appointment the following Wednesday to go in to the Ruby store she had made several purchases at to do an audit to determine whether the store was following her new return procedure. She had decided, with Mr. Brown's approval, that she would take a longer lunch hour to do her audit. The store personnel would be unaware of who she was and what she would be looking for.

After entering Ruby's, she pretended to be shopping while keeping her eye on the cash and wrap area. She hoped to observe someone coming in to return an item. The new procedure that she had put into effect was that the head cashier doing the return would call management or another employee to come to the register and verify that there was a customer requesting a return, check the item being returned, and witness the return as it was being performed by signing the return form once the transaction was completed, thereby implementing a check-and-balance system. She was relieved when it wasn't long before a customer came in to do a return. Hannah was satisfied when she heard the cashier paging the manager on duty to come up and observe the return. If the store continued this practice, it would soon eliminate a lot of the cash shortages that had occurred previously.

The second part of her return procedure was a little more complicated and required an outside party to perform it. This is where she came in and where Harley expressed his worry and apprehension over her having to do it. Nevertheless, Hannah requested that one of the cashiers call for the manager, and she patiently waited.

Once the manager arrived, Hannah said, "Hello, Cindy," quickly reading her name tag, "I am Hannah North. Drew Williams should have advised you that I would be coming by today. Can we go to the office?"

She was pleased to see that Cindy knew about her coming and had her follow her to the back of the store where the office was located. Once inside the office, Hannah said, "I am here to review the return slips for the past week. Will you get them for me?"

"Of course," Cindy responded. She watched as Cindy reached for the stack of return slips and handed them over.

"I know as a store manager you are very busy and must have a million things to do. You can go out on the floor for now, and if I need you, I will come and get you." She was relieved to see Cindy leave and hurried to start reviewing the return slips. Part of her check-and-balance procedure, was to go into the stores and randomly choose several return slips and call the customer to follow up while verifying if they were legitimate returns. In her previous management assignment, she had discovered that fraudulent returns were being done in order to steal money. She was hoping this wouldn't be the case with the Ruby stores, but this would be a way to discover if there was a problem.

"Who was that that went into the office with Cindy?" John asked Candy, the cashier who had paged the manager.

"How would I know?" Candy stated.

"Well, I need you to find out. She acts like she's snooping, and I don't like it," John replied angrily.

"I heard her say her name was Hannah North, but that's all I know." They were interrupted when a customer came to the register to make a purchase. "Did you find everything okay today?" Candy asked.

John had a bad feeling and wasn't liking all the new changes that were happening at Ruby's. He felt sure Hannah must have something to do with it all, and he was determined to find out. He and the former head cashier, Mandy, had made extra money on the side, and he was hurting for money now that she was no longer employed. She had claimed that someone had ratted her out, and he had a feeling it was this Hannah North person!

Hannah had a few more returns to call on and was feeling good so far that all the returns had been legitimate. As she reviewed the remaining slips, she noticed that one of the slips was completed by the former head cashier, Mandy, and verified by another person named John. She decided this would be a good one to audit and dialed the number listed on the paper. The call was answered by a recording advising the number was no longer in service. She looked at the cash amount and saw that it was a transaction for forty dollars in art supplies. A red flag immediately went up, and she decided she needed to see if there were any more return slips completed by Mandy and John.

She found two more in the stack, and when she dialed the phone number on the next slip, she got the recording again advising the number was no longer in service. This transaction was for fifty dollars in floral supplies. When she called on the last return slip, she did reach a customer. The customer let her know that they had never been in a Ruby's store, and they didn't have time to answer any questions. This transaction was for seventy dollars and listed art supplies as well as frames. Hannah went over to the copy machine and made copies of the three return slips that looked fraudulent and immediately tucked them away in her purse. She returned the stack of slips to Cindy's desk and left the office.

John was in the back of the store waiting and watching for Hannah. He wanted to make sure that he got a good look at her, and if time permitted, he would leave the store and try to follow her. He watched her as she approached Cindy, and he tried to stay within listening distance of their conversation.

"I finished my review and left the return slips on your desk, Cindy."

"Did everything go okay?" Cindy asked.

"I will send my report to Drew, and if there are any questions or problems, he'll get in touch with you. Thank you for your help."

"No problem," Cindy replied, watching Hannah leave the store.

"I'm taking my lunch hour now," John informed Cindy as he rushed to follow Hannah out the door.

Hannah got into her silver Toyota Camry and decided to go home for lunch so she could reassure Harley she was okay. She was lost in thought about her audit and didn't really notice the brown truck following her.

John smiled when he saw Hannah turn into her driveway and watched as the garage door opened permitting her car to enter. "It's nice to know where you live, lady, in case you cause me any problems and I need to come and see you."

Chapter 15

A few days had gone by since Hannah had informed Drew of her findings on the return slips. Drew had told her it made perfect sense with the shortages that were occurring in that particular Ruby's store. She didn't envy his job of having to confront another dishonest employee.

On the positive side, Hannah had received an extra thousand dollars in income for her detective work at Ruby's that week, and the added income would help relieve a big burden of stress with living on such a strict budget. She thought Harley would be thrilled when she told him about the extra income; however, he still moped around the house like he had lost his best friend.

"Harley, I thought you would be happy about the extra money we just made. That means more yummy treats for you and extra food for me. Although I do have to admit my figure hasn't looked this good in years with the diet I've been on. I might be better off staying on this diet. What do you think, Harley?"

"Meow."

"What kind of response was that, Harley? Are you feeling okay? You seem to have lost your zest for anything lately! Do I need to take you to the vet?"

"MEOW!"

"That's better. For a minute, you really had me worried! I'm going to go and get ready for my date with Drew."

"Meow."

Harley watched Hannah go upstairs and decided while Hannah was out on her date, he would go and talk to Rocky and Fluffy. He had an uneasy feeling that something was going to happen, and he wanted to be prepared for whatever was coming his way.

* * * * *

Hannah and Drew decided they would go for a walk after enjoying dinner together. "You seem to be lost in thought tonight, Hannah. Is everything okay?"

"I'm worried about Harley. He hasn't been himself lately, and I'm not sure what's going on with him. Ever since I wrote the new policies for Ruby's, he's been very agitated and upset. He thinks I'm going to get hurt."

"He actually told you that?" Drew asked with surprise.

"Well, it's kind of hard to explain but not in so many words. Harley has been my only companion for so many years, that I can just tell what he's thinking by his moods, the way he meows, and his body language. I hope you don't think I'm crazy. Animals love me, and I've always had this ability to communicate with them on a different level. I guess that's the best way of putting it," Hannah replied, hoping that Drew wouldn't run for the hills now that she had shared a hidden secret about herself.

"I just didn't realize it was possible. I will admit this, Harley's not just any cat. He's my buddy now, and I'm growing quite fond of him."

"I'm so glad you two are getting along so well. That's so important to me. I know that Harley loves it when you call him BIG guy. Drew, tell me more about what happened with John…if you feel comfortable talking about it."

"John is definitely a piece of work. He, of course, blamed everything on Mandy, claiming he had nothing to do with any of it. I have dealt with his type before, and he is not a good employee, in my opinion. He has been placed on probation with limited hours and will be watched. We're actually hoping the probation and limited hours will be enough to get him to quit and go somewhere else."

"That is the downside of being in loss prevention and management. You sure don't win any popularity contests!" Hannah said on a lighter note.

"Well, I do hope I'm winning a popularity contest with you," Drew said while pulling her close and kissing her tenderly. "I'm glad our paths crossed, and it's times like this that I'm grateful to have someone as special as you are to share things with."

* * * * *

Harley had just finished meeting with Rocky and Fluffy, and they had both agreed to stand watch. He just had a feeling that something bad was going to happen, and he wanted to be ready.

"Good night, Drew. Thank you for another wonderful evening. See you soon!" Hannah waved and watched Drew climb into his convertible. She closed the door and began securing her home for the night. "Did you have a good night, Harley?"

"Meow."

Hannah was walking to turn off the kitchen light when there was a knock on the front door. Turning, she said to Harley, "I wonder if Drew forgot something."

When she opened the door, an angry boy pushed his way inside. "So, you must be the almighty Hannah North."

"I don't know about almighty, but I am Hannah North. And you are?" Hannah asked, trying to stay calm.

"John…the one you're trying to blame for all the shortages at Ruby's!"

"So why are you here, John?"

"I think you need to be taught a lesson!"

John was interrupted by a deadly warning growl, and when he turned to see where the noise was coming from, he saw Harley getting ready to pounce.

"What the—" John yelled in surprise. He quickly grabbed Hannah's arm, forcing her toward the door. He managed to get her outside and continued to push her down the front steps while heading in the direction of his truck.

Harley was able to slip through the door when John opened it and raced to signal Rocky and Fluffy. Within minutes, his team was on the scene, and Rocky took the lead, tackling John to the ground. Hannah was able to get away and ran into the house to call the police. She could hear John screaming for help and smiled with relief when she realized how fortunate she was to have such an amazing team protecting her.

The police arrived within minutes, and Hannah was thrilled to see Officers Grant and Sheldon. "Looks like you did it again, Hannah! Who did your remarkable team snatch this time?"

"Well, it's kind of a long story…" Hannah began but quickly explained about the cash shortages at Ruby's and John's involvement. "I will give you the name and phone number of Ruby's loss prevention agent, and he can provide any more details you might need. As for my team getting involved, they are always worried about keeping me safe, and I have to say, I'm very glad they were on duty tonight!"

She winked at Harley and gave him the thumbs-up sign. She could tell Harley was proud of his team, even Rocky with all his drool. After winking her approval at him, she noticed he signaled his team to follow him to the backyard, and she was sure he would be promising them treats tomorrow.

* * * * *

Several hours later, Hannah lovingly patted Harley's head when they were sitting on her bed and said, "Have I told you lately what an amazing kitty you are?"

"Meow."

"You saved my life tonight. Thank you, Harley dog."

"Meow."

"We are definitely a team, and I couldn't do it without you!"

"Meow."

"From now on, I will always trust your intuition. Good thing you're my partner! You are still my partner, right?"

"Meow."

"Do you want to stay in the investigation business, or have you had enough?"

"Meow…meow."

"Okay, partner….Here's to many more crimes to be solved. To Hannah and Harley, a.k.a. H & H Investigations!"

"Meow!"

Ingram Content Group UK Ltd.
Milton Keynes UK
UKHW010846020723
424411UK00007B/274